I0634365

Lucy Ellen Guernsey

A Lent In Earnest

Lucy Ellen Guernsey

A Lent In Earnest

ISBN/EAN: 9783741193538

Manufactured in Europe, USA, Canada, Australia, Japa

Cover: Foto ©Andreas Hilbeck / pixelio.de

Manufactured and distributed by brebook publishing software
(www.brebook.com)

Lucy Ellen Guernsey

A Lent In Earnest

ASH WEDNESDAY.

THE key-notes of the services for Ash Wednesday are repentance and confession. Theirs is the spirit of the first collect, of the prayers which, in the American service for the day, follow the Litany, of the portion appointed for the Epistle, and of the Lessons, "That we, worthily lamenting our sins, and acknowledging our wretchedness;" "Turn Thine anger from us who meekly acknowledge our vileness." "Be favorable to thy people who turn to Thee in weeping, fasting, and praying."

We often use words, even very common words, without any clear or exact idea of their meaning. "I know, but I cannot tell," is an expression familiar to every teacher. Now the truth is, we cannot be quite sure whether we know or not, unless we try to put our knowledge into words. Let us, then, examine a little our ideas on this very important matter.

7

We find these two duties of repentance and confession constantly conjoined in both the Old and New Testaments. The Psalms are full of them. " I acknowledge my transgression, and my sin is ever before me." (Ps. li. 3.) " Heal my soul, for I have sinned against Thee ! (Ps. xli. 4.) " Repent, and turn yourselves from all your transgression, so iniquity shall not be your ruin." (Ezek. xviii. 30.) Our Lord's own preaching began with repentance, as did that of His fore-runner, John the Baptist. (S. Matt. iii. 2 ; S. Mark i. 15.) It was the first commission of the Apostles (S. Mark vi. 12), as it was the burden of their preaching after the day of Pentecost. (Acts ii. 38.)

So with confession. We read in Lev. xxvii 40-42, after the most terrible denunciations of woe against the chosen people in case of unfaithfulness, these reassuring words: "If they will confess their iniquity and the iniquity of their fathers, if, then, their uncircumcised heart be humbled, and they accept the punishment of their iniquity, then will I remember my covenant with Jacob! " So in Psalm xxxii. 5; Joel ii. 12; 1 John i. 9, and many other places.

Our Church, too, in all her services, constantly presses these-things on our attention. Since, then, they are so important, is it not very needful that our ideas about them should be clear and definite, free from mistake or haziness? What, then, are repentance and confession?

Repentance, as the word is used in the service for Ash Wednesday, and generally in the Bible and the Prayer-book, means turning *from* sin, and *to* God. It has another meaning in some places—that of sorrow or regret, as in Gen. vi. 6. "And it repented the Lord that He had made man." But in general, it means such sorrow for sin as leads to the forsaking of it. A man may be sorry for some transgression because it has led him into trouble; as when a drunkard has destroyed his health, or a thief has brought himself into the grasp of the law; but such sorrow cannot properly be called repentance. The sinner does not hate the sin. On the contrary, he loves it, and is only sorry that he has put it out of his power to commit it again.

But true repentance means sorrow for sin, because that sin has broken God's law, and grieved and offended Him. It means a steadfast determination to give up everything which our own conscience or the law of God shows us to be wrong. " Repent, and turn yourselves from *all* your transgressions." (Ezek. xviii. 30.) Observe the word ALL. It will not do to keep anything back, to have any little secret shrine, in which is hidden an idol. God is a discerner of the thoughts and intents of the heart. (Rom. vi. 12.) The darkness of its most secret inner chamber is no darkness to Him, and He will endure no willful deceit in this matter.

I say *willful* deceit, because we may unconsciously deceive ourselves, especially in the beginning of our religious lives. As we advance in holiness, we shall no doubt see many things to be wrong which did not seem so at first. But true repentance does require that we give up everything that we know, or even suspect, to be wrong.

Nor can this work of repentance be finished up in one day, or one Lenten season. It will have to be renewed again and again, so long as we inhabit these mortal bodies; as often as we are made conscious that we have offended by thought, word, or deed against the Divine Majesty. We must remember that our Heavenly Father's precious promises of remission and forgiveness are made only to penitent sinners. "Repent, and be baptized," said St. Peter to the inquirers on the day of Pentecost, and again, in his second sermon, "Repent ye, therefore, and be converted, that your sins may be blotted out when the times of refreshing shall come from the presence of the Lord." (Acts ii. 38, and iii. 19.) The prodigal son, in the midst of his wandering and wickedness, was no doubt an object of love and care to his father, but it was not till he returned to his father's house, and submitted to his authority, that he was restored to favor. Not that there is any merit in repentance, as if we thereby earned a title to forgiveness: we must not entertain for a moment any such idea as that. Salvation is, in its very nature, a deliverance from sin. That is what it means. But unless we see the evil of sin we shall not wish to be delivered from it. Therefore, in every case, the first direction to the inquirer is " Repent."

But of what are we to repent ?

Of all our wrong doing and thinking and feeling—of our neglect of God and His service—of our carelessness in this most important concern of life—of all our evil deeds and thoughts and tempers. The more closely we examine ourselves by the light of God's Word, the more we shall see to deplore, till we come at last to know practically what we have perhaps always believed as a doctrine— that in us, that is, in our flesh, dwelleth no good thing, and that not only man in general, but we ourselves, are prone to evil as the sparks fly upward.

Let us not, therefore, be discouraged, or faint in our minds! For all this evil the remedy is provided. Hear what comfortable words the Scripture hath for our encouragement. "Jesus Christ came into the world to save sinners." (1 Tim. i. 15.) "I am not come to call the righteous, but sinners to repentance." (S. Matt. ix. 13.) Take your reference Bible and look up the passages relating to this subject, and you will see that there is no room for discouragement, much less for despair.

Ps. li.   S. Luke xv. 1–10.

FIRST THURSDAY IN LENT.

CONFESSION.

IN many places of Scripture, we find coupled with repentance another condition of repentance—that is, confession. "I acknowledged my sin unto Thee, and mine iniquity have I not hid. I said, I will confess my sins unto the Lord, and so Thou forgavest the iniquity of my sin." (Ps. xxxii. 5.) "Only acknowledge thine iniquity that thou hast sinned against the Lord." (Jer. iii. 13.) "If we confess our sins, God is faithful and just to forgive us our sins, and to cleanse us from all unrighteousness." (1 John i. 9.)

To whom are we to confess ?

First of all, to ourselves. We are frankly to acknowledge our iniquity, and that not in general terms alone, but we are to come down to particulars. It is easy to own ourselves sinners in a general way, while all the time we are cherishing a very good opinion of ourselves. "Oh, yes, we are all miserable sinners!" said a shrewd old lady ; "but we are just as good as the rest of the miserable sinners, and a good deal better than some of them." I fancy we all have this feeling at times, though we may not put it to ourselves quite so plainly.

In order to make our confession to ourselves of any use, it must be frank and open. It will not do to accompany every confession with an excuse. " I spoke hastily and unkindly, but then I had great provocation." "I ought not to have repeated that scandalous story, but then I had it on good authority." "I ought perhaps to have abstained from that amusement, but A and B went, and I do not pretend to be better than they." Have we not all excused ourselves in this style again and again? But what is this but saying that we should never do wrong if we were never tempted? Let us consider whether we dare offer these excuses to God before we venture to comfort and quiet our own consciences with them!

Secondly, we must confess our sins unto the LORD. " I said, I will confess my sin unto the Lord." (Ps. xxxii. 5.) " Take with you words, and turn unto the Lord." (Hos. xiv. 2.)

"But," you say, "does He not already

know my sins? Why, then, should I confess them?" In the first place, because He has seen fit to command it. He also knows all our wants and wishes far better than we ourselves ; yet He has commanded us in everything to make known our requests to Him. " Be careful for nothing, but in everything by prayer and supplication, with thanksgiving let your requests be made known unto God." (Phil. iv. 6.) Surely His will should be enough for us, since He commands nothing without good cause.

But, secondly, we should confess our sins to God, because in that way alone can we be made thoroughly aware of their sinfulness. A fit of causeless anger, or a bit of malicious gossip, looks very different to us when we lay it bare before God in our closets. The excuse which seemed very plausible when the act was committed, will not appear so in the light of His presence before whom we stand, and who is of purer eyes than to behold iniquity. If we are honest in our confession, the Spirit, which searcheth all things, will show us aggravations of our fault which we never suspected.

Finally, we should confess our sin unto the Lord for the sake of the peace which the action brings to our own hearts and minds. There is no time when our conscience torments us so sorely as when we are trying to persuade ourselves that it is not hurting us at all ; when we are making all sorts of excuses to ourselves for our faults.

A wise and witty man once said that all the riches and pleasures which life has to offer would be embittered and made useless to a man who was compelled always to wear a sharp nail in his shoe. No doubt, he was right. Now, an unconfessed, and, therefore, unforgiven, sin is just such a nail. It is true that by a long course of neglect the conscience may be silenced for a time. But it is only for a time, and how awful will be the awaking!

Let us, then, come boldly but humbly to the Throne of Grace—to the Mercy-seat, where our God is always to be found by those who honestly seek Him! Let us confess all those sins which, by our frailty, we have committed, and ask for forgiveness and cleansing for His sake by whose stripes we are healed, who bore our sins in His own body on the tree, and who now sits at the right hand of the Father to make intercession for us. Let us do so, not trusting in ourselves as if there were any merit in the act, but trusting alone in His gracious promises, and we shall find peace to our souls.

Psalm xxxii.   1 John i.

FIRST FRIDAY IN LENT.

FORGIVENESS.

HAVING, then, come to the Throne of Grace with true repentance and humble confession, let us not fail to accept the promises of God in all their fullness. Too many do this, and even value themselves on what they term humility, but which is in reality faithlessness. "I should never dare to believe that my sins were really forgiven," said a certain person; "I should think it presumption." Now which is the greater presumption, to believe what God says, or to disbelieve it? See how full and explicit are His words of promise to all who turn to Him! "If we confess our sins, He is faithful and just to forgive us our sins, and to cleanse us from all unrighteousness." (1 John i. 19.) Observe the fullness and force of the promise: He is faithful and just. Faithful, because He has promised; just, because our Lord has borne our sins in His own body on the tree (I Pet. ii. 24), and has suffered, the just for the unjust. (I Pet. iii. 18.)

Nor is this all. He not only forgives our sin, but he washes it away, and makes it as if it had never been. "Though your sins be as scarlet, they shall be as white as snow; though they be red like crimson, they shall be as wool." (Is. i. 18.) "The blood of Jesus Christ cleanseth us from all sin." (I John i. 17.)

We must never suffer ourselves to doubt, much less to despair of God's mercy. Such doubts are amongst Satan's favorite weapons. "How many times have you asked forgiveness for this very sin already," he whispers; "How many times have you professed repentance, and promised never to commit it more? Is it not presumption, yea, mockery, to ask God to forgive you again?" Do not for a moment listen to him. What are you going to do if you do not ask? You will certainly never be rid of your sin in any other way than by God's help, and how are you to obtain that help but by coming to Him? He who bade us forgive an erring brother, not seven times, but seventy times seven, is not

likely to be less merciful Himself. "There is
more grace in God than there is sin in all the
sinners that ever lived," said an aged saint
of God when this matter was under discus-
sion; and he was right. But are we not in
danger of presumption in thus believing that
God is ready to forgive, however many times
we sin against Him? Not if we are sincere
and honest in our repentance, and in our
hatred of sin. It would, indeed, be the greatest of presumption to go cn willfully indulging in sin on such grounds. The person who
did so would be a hypocrite. His repentance would be no more than a pretence,
and his profession a mockery and a lie. But
to the honest penitent, I believe nothing
can be more calculated to humble him in the
very dust with a sense of his own unworthiness than the conviction that, after all his
vileness and ingratitude, his Heavenly Father
has pardoned him, and taken him again into
favor. "And I will establish my covenant
with thee, and thou shalt know that I am
the Lord," says God to the rebellious and
polluted daughter of Jerusalem, after enum-
erating all her horrible offenses; and He
adds these significant words: "That thou
mayest remember, and be confounded, and

never open thy mouth any more, when I am pacified towards thee for all the evil that thou hast done, saith the Lord." (Ezek. xvi. 63.)

Shall we, in the face of such gracious and glorious promises as these, dare to doubt the goodness and mercy of our Father ? Shall we bring the burden of our sins to Him who has covenanted by His justice, as well as by His mercy and love, to blot out our transgressions for His own sake, and not remember our sins, and then take up that burden and carry it away again ? Shall our doubts make Him a liar ? Surely, this is presumption, and not the humble faith which trusts in Him, and takes Him at His word. Let us then rejoice in the belief that our Heavenly Father has pardoned and cleansed us according to His immutable word—that our unrighteousness is forgiven and our sin is covered, and that to us the Lord does not impute sin. (Ps. xxxii. 1, 2.) So shall we find that peace which the world knows not, and can never know, and that joy in which it has no part. So shall we have all our wounds healed, and find strength to fight the good fight of faith in the time to come. " For the joy of the Lord is your strength." (Neh. viii. 10.)

Psalm xxxii.   1 John.

FIRST SATURDAY IN LENT.

CONSECRATION.

WHAT is consecration ?

It is setting apart. When a building, as a church, is consecrated to the worship of God, we understand that it is set apart for His worship, and is not to be put to any other use. When a bishop is consecrated, he is set apart from worldly business for his sacred office, and he is expected to give up all his time and talents to the duties of that office.

In the same way, a truly consecrated Christian is one who has given himself up wholly to the service of God, his Creator, Redeemer, and Sanctifier — who aims to please not himself, but God, in all he says, does, and thinks. His time, his talents, his worldly goods, his position and influence, his very amusements, are used for the service of God, and he is ready to give up his most cherished pursuit as soon as he is made aware that it is not pleasing to his Heavenly Master.

We find in Holy Scripture abundant war-
rant for such consecration. " What, know
ye not that your body is the temple of the
Holy Ghost which is in you, which ye have
of God ? And ye are not your own, for ye
are bought with a price; therefore glorify
God in your bodies, and in your spirits, which
are His." (1 Cor. vi. 19, 20.) " For no man
liveth to himself, and no man dieth to himself. For whether we live, we live unto the
Lord, and whether we die, we die unto the
Lord. Whether we live, therefore, or die, we
are the Lord's." (Rom. xiv. 7, 8.) In this
chapter, be it observed, the Apostle is speaking of so common a matter as eating and
drinking, and he says, again, " Whether ye
eat or drink, or whatever ye do, do all to
the glory of God." (1 Cor. x. 31.) Again,
" I beseech you, brethren, by the mercies of
God, that ye present your bodies a living
sacrifice, holy, acceptable unto God, which
is your reasonable service." (Rom. xii. 1.)

The Church teaches us the same lesson in
her most solemn act of worship. " And
here we offer and present unto Thee, O
Lord, ourselves, our souls and bodies," is
the language of the prayer of consecration
in the office of the Holy Communion. The

same thought is found repeated again and again in the Prayer-book, notably in the collects for the fourth and fifth Sundays after Easter. Every Communion Sunday, if we are worthy communicants, we make, or rather renew, this consecration of ourselves to our Lord.

But in order to make this consecration acceptable to God, or useful to ourselves, it must be entire and perfect. We must not follow the example of Ananias and Sapphira, in professing to give all, and then keeping back a part. So long as we "keep back part of the price," so long as we hold fast to anything we know we ought to give up, or hold ourselves back from any duty we know we ought to perform, so long is our offering imperfect—unpleasing to God, and unprofitable to ourselves. "Cursed be the deceiver that hath in his flock a male, and voweth and sacrificeth to the Lord a corrupt thing," said the prophet to the Jews after the captivity. (Mal. i. 14.) Their God had redeemed them from captivity worse than death, had brought them to their own land once more, and restored to them their old religious privileges, yet they reckoned His service weariness, and grudged to give of their best for

His offering. Our Lord has redeemed us from a worse bondage than theirs, and has bought us with a great price, even with the suffering and death of His dear Son, and shall we grudge to give Him that which is His own?

The want of this perfect consecration is the reason why so many Christian people have no comfort in their devotion. Old-fashioned Methodist people used to employ a significant phrase in this connection. They would ask, " Do you enjoy religion?" Too many, it is to be feared, do not enjoy it at all. They seem to have just enough to make them uncomfortable. "I feel as if it were of no use for me to pray," said one; " my prayers never seem to get out of the room, and my heart is cold and heavy. I have no sense of the Lord's presence at all." " Are you sure," asked her friend, "that you are indulging no sin, or neglecting no known duty?" After a moment's pause came the question, "Do you think such a thing is wrong?" "Whatever I think, I know what *you* think," was her friend's inward answer.

Our God is a jealous God! He will not share His temple with another. If we would have Him dwelling in our hearts, we must banish thence every idol, and every unclean and even doubtful thing. For we must remember that if we think any act wrong, or even doubtful, that act becomes a sin to us. This is true especially of amusements and pleasures of all sorts. He who risks God's anger for the sake of a personal gratification, is guilty of presumptuous sin.

If, then, you find your religious state unsatisfactory, your prayers lifeless, your sacramental seasons without comfort or enjoyment, your heart heavy under a secret sense of condemnation, let me beg you to examine yourself, and see if the trouble does not lie just here—that you are keeping back something that your Lord requires of you. And if, on an honest search, you find that He calls on you to give up some indulgence to which you are holding fast, or to take up some duty which you have hitherto neglected, let me beg of you to obey on the instant; whatever be the cost, break the idol, banish the intruder, take up the duty, and, so doing, find peace to your soul.

Mal. i.   Rom. xii.

FIRST SUNDAY IN LENT.

FASTING.

THE special service for this day sets before us, as the subject of our meditation, our Lord's fast in the wilderness. The collect is founded on it. " O Lord, who for our sakes didst fast forty days!" The Gospel for the day sets forth the story of the same fast, and of the temptation which followed.

It was for our sake that the Blessed Jesus fasted. His sinless nature had no need of such discipline. But He was " to be tempted in all points like as we are," that we might know that " we have not a High Priest who cannot be touched with the feeling of our infirmities." (Heb. iv. 15.) " For in that He Himself hath suffered being tempted, He is able to succor them that are tempted." (Heb. ii. 18.) Let us, with reverence and godly fear, consider a few of the circumstances of His fasting and temptation.

It was immediately after our Lord's baptism, and the wonderful manifestation of the Divine Glory in confirmation of His claims, that He was "led up of the Spirit into the wilderness to be tempted of the Devil." After the privilege came the temptation. If we consider our own experience, we shall often find this to be the case with ourselves. How often, after a season of more than usual earnestness and enjoyment in devotion, does the heart seem to go back with a rebound, as it were, to the vanities of the world! How often, after an act of honest renunciation, does the thing we have given up paint itself to our fancy in more attractive colors than ever, till we think ourselves little better than hypocrites, and are ready to give up in despair!

But we have no reason to despair. Nay, we may, if we use them aright, make our very temptations means of grace, drawing from them both encouragement and strength—encouragement, because Satan would not take so much pains to draw us aside if he did not see that we were escaping from his power; strength, if we let our trials make us more watchful against sin, and more earnest in our prayers for help.

Our Lord's first temptation came through

the medium of His bodily wants.   He was exhausted from fasting; and Satan, as is usual with him, attacked him on what he believed his weak point.   " If thou be the Son of God, command that these stones be made bread."   (S. Matt. iv. 3.)   He often assaults us in the same way.   " You are tired and hungry," he says; " you have a right to be irritable."   " You are an invalid; you have the right to be exacting, and to make the comfort of others give way to yours."   " You are sleepless, and in pain ; you have a right to take the drug which will give you present ease and rest, whatever may be the consequence."   Let us answer as did our Lord: " Man shall not live by bread alone."   Let us remember that the body is to be the servant, not the master, and treat it accordingly.   There are no persons who need to practice self-control more than invalids, and especially nervous invalids.

Again, our Lord did not make use of His divine power against the tempter.   He used weapons which are within the reach of every one of us.   He met Satan with the words of Holy Scripture.   And in this very fact, by the way, may be found an answer to those who decry and undervalue the Old Testament. Every one of our Lord's quotations is taken from the book of Deuteronomy. And we may furnish ourselves, if we will, with weapons from the same celestial armory. Does Satan attack us through our bodily weakness? "My grace is sufficient for thee, for my strength is made perfect in weakness." (2 Cor. xii. 9.) Does he beset us with doubts as to the forgiveness of our sins, or acceptance with God? Every disciple has, like Christian in the Pilgrim's Progress, "a key in his bosom, which will open any lock in Doubting Castle." Hence the importance of making ourselves very familiar with the weapons which St. Paul calls "the sword of the Spirit," and of having it, as it were, always at our side. A man might have the best weapon in the world in his possession, but it would stand him in little stead when attacked, if he did not know how to use it, or if he had left it hanging up in his closet at home. But if we store our memories with the very words of the Bible, and meditate often thereon, we shall have sword and shield always at hand. I shall have more to say on this matter hereafter.

Once more, temptation, valorously withstood, is followed by peace. "Then the

Devil leaveth Him, and behold, angels came, and ministered unto Him." (S. Matt. iv. 11.) "Our Lord will not suffer us to be tempted above that we are able." (1 Cor. x. 18.) Satan may rage, but his rage is restrained by one stronger than he, and after the storm comes a calm. Then come to us, as to the pilgrim, some of the leaves of the tree of life, to heal our wounds, and if the white robe has contracted any stain in the strife, there is opened the fountain for sin and uncleanness, where we may wash and be clean. (Zech. xiii. 1.) We must still be on our guard, and have our weapons at hand, but our Captain allows us a breathing-time, and He will himself come and talk with us as we rest by the way.

 Ps. xlvi.   S. Matt. iii.

FIRST MONDAY IN LENT.

FASTING.

WHAT is fasting?

In its broadest sense it is self-denial. As generally used by our Church, it means abstinence in some shape — either from amusement, from food, or from personal luxuries. The Romish Church makes it to consist mostly in refraining from meat, especially during Lent; but that is a narrow view of the matter, and one which admits of a great deal of personal indulgence. The early Church made no distinction in quality of food, and the most scrupulous did not hesitate to eat meat when needful. Our own branch of the Church lays down no definite rules on the subject of fasting, either in Lent or at any other time, but, with her usual wisdom and liberality, leaves the matter to each person's conscience.

It has been remarked that there is no absolute command to fast in the New Testament. Our Lord, however, implicitly sanctions and approves the practice by His example, and by giving directions as to how the duty is to be performed (S. Matt. vi. 16), and by His words to the Pharisees (S. Mark ii. 19) ; and it is commended by the practice of the Apostles. (Acts xiii. 2, 3, and xiv. 23.) Our Lord tells us that fasting, like prayer, should be performed without ostentation, and this is the only direction given on the subject.

The law of Moses appoints only one fast,

that of the great day of atonement (Lev. xxiii. 27), but we find in the Old Testament numerous examples of fasts, usually on occasion of some great danger or calamity (2 Chron. xx. 3; Joel ii), or of some dangerous enterprise. In the writings of the prophets, also, we find many allusions to fasting as a common practice, and also directions as to the spirit in which it should be performed.

Our Church observes all Fridays throughout the year as fast days, and also the forty days before Easter. This last season, called Lent (probably from the Saxon word for Spring), is that with which we are specially concerned at present. How, then, shall we keep Lent ?

The Church answers this question, to some extent, by her multiplied services and frequent Communions — by the opportunities which she gives us of social worship. Let us avail ourselves of this privilege as far as possible, by being frequently in the sanctuary, and by joining heartily in the prayers and praises of God's people. Let us be early in our places, that our spirits may be quieted, and our hearts attuned by some minutes of prayer and meditation, before the service begins.

The quiet and the association of the place are specially favorable to such exercises. Many people find an advantage in reading some devotional book at this time, such as Thomas à Kempis, or the Sacra Privata, and this is a good plan, provided always that the book be used as a guide to meditation, and not as a substitute for it. As a rule, we read too much and think too little.

Our prayers should be not only for ourselves, but for our fellow-worshippers, and for all the interests of our own Church and the Church at large. Let us remember our families, the guild or society to which we belong, our god-children and pupils in Sunday-school, the missionary enterprises of our own parish and those of the Church. We shall find that a few minutes spent in this way, on entering church, will compose our minds, and add tenfold to the comfort and usefulness of the service which follows.

Many sincere Christians are troubled with wandering thoughts in time of prayer, and especially of public service. I have always found great assistance in keeping my eyes fixed on the book, following every word of the service. Such wandering thoughts are like dogs which run out and bark at us in the street—the best way is to go straight on and take no notice of them. But as an old author has said, the best way to govern our thoughts in prayer is to be in the habit of governing them at all other times.

When service is over, let us not be in a hurry to rise from our knees, but let us again spend a few moments in secret devotion. I much like the custom of the congregation remaining in their seats or standing till the minister leaves the chancel. And let us strive, above all, to carry with us through the day the influence of the blessed services in which we have been engaged. The Psalms or the Lessons will have furnished us with some food for meditation, to which our minds may turn in the intervals of business, and from which we may draw counsel and comfort, and

"at evening we may say,
I have walked with God to-day."

Is. lxiii.　　　　　　　　S. Mark vi.

FIRST TUESDAY IN LENT.

HOW SHALL WE KEEP LENT?

YOU say, perhaps, "I am shut up—confined to the room or the house," or, "I am away from the church and its worship. I cannot join in the services, however much I should like to do so."

This is a mistake, and a very unfortunate one, which is likely to deprive the person making it of much spiritual growth as well as comfort. No one needs the helps which the Church holds out to her children more than those who are shut away from the more public means of grace. We are too apt to think of the Church, not as the one Body of Christ, but as a mass of disconnected parishes and individuals. You are as much a member of the Church at large when you are a thousand miles away from her services, or when you are kept helpless on your bed, as though you were in the heart of a great cathedral city, with opportunities of attending a grand service every day.

It is one of the blessings of our inestimable book of Common Prayer that it enables us to join in the prayers and praises of those who are able to attend public worship. If from illness or any other cause you are kept from going to church, let me ask you to take the Prayer-book, and follow the service in your own room. Read the proper Psalms and Lessons, and, that you may do so, keep yourself in mind of all the Church days and seasons. This is easily done in these days of cheap almanacs and wall calendars. Do not, if you can help it, let one day pass without reading at least one of the proper Lessons for the day, and one of the Psalms, and using some part of the appointed prayers. You will never appreciate as you should the wonderful beauty of our service, and its suitableness to your spiritual needs, till you learn to use it in your private devotions.

But in order to this appreciation, we must guard against formality, and carelessness. Let us study the service, and commit it to memory; especially the collects, those wonderful jewels of devotion, which shine the more the more they are looked at and used. I can testify, from my own experience, to the value of this practice to the sick and feeble.

Many times, when oppressed by pain and weakness, or vexed and distracted by nervous irritation, unable to frame a sentence, or to put even into thought the desires and griefs of a burdened heart, have I found unspeakable comfort and help in the dear, familiar words which came almost without an effort, and expressed the longings of my soul better than any words of my own.

Let me beg of you, then, dear shut-in and shut-out brothers and sisters, to make bosom friends and companions of your prayer-books. Let them be always at hand, and never, if you can help it, omit using a part at least of the service for the day. This will require some effort and self-denial, but this very effort and self-denial will do you good, and are exercises most suitable to the season.

Believe me, if you will but follow the practice through one Lenten season, you will never again willingly omit it.

Ps. lxxxiv.   Eph. iv. 1-17.

SECOND WEDNESDAY IN·LENT.

ABSTINENCE.

WE have already seen that fasting, in its broad sense, means self-denial, and in the ordinary sense, abstinence. In this latter sense it is used in the collect for the day. Now abstinence, we all know, means " going without something," and the question to be settled by each one of us is, " What shall we do without ? "

The Church, always discreet and liberal in her requirements, lays down no rules in this matter, but leaves it to the judgment and conscience of each individual of her children. We are to be, not without law, but a law unto ourselves. One may abstain in matters of food, another of some favorite occupation or amusement, such, for instance, as light reading or fancy work, or a favorite game. Another will take time from his business or pleasure for devotional reading, or for some work of charity.

We are to be a law unto ourselves, but let

our rule *be* a law. Do not let the matter be left to chance, or the impulse of the moment. "Let every man be fully persuaded in his own mind," said St. Paul, speaking of a somewhat similar matter. (Rom. xiv. 5.) He is writing to the Christians of Rome, many of whom had been Jews, and still found their consciences burdened at times by the requirements of ceremonial law. "One," he says, "believeth that he may eat all things; another, who is weak, eateth only herbs; one esteemeth one day above another; another esteemeth every day alike." But however that might be, every one was enjoined to be "fully persuaded in his own mind," and not to act against that persuasion—that is, against the leading of his own conscience.

Having, then, laid down a rule—having decided on that measure of abstinence which we deem best for ourselves—let us adhere to that standard, however we may be tempted to depart from it. For instance, if you decide to give some particular part of the day to devotional reading or study—a very excellent practice—do not let every little matter, especially of your own convenience, divert you from your object. If you decide to abstain from light reading, hold fast to your

resolution in the face of the most fascinating
and bepraised novel. Unless you do thus
adhere to them, your rules will be burdens
and temptations instead of helps.

There is another and a very important
point to be considered in this matter of
amusements. In the very chapter that we
have been quoting, St. Paul says: "If meat
make my brother to offend, I will eat no
meat while the world stands." The church
man or woman who is seen at the opera or
theatre during Lent must not be surprised
if he hears his religious profession lightly
spoken of by worldly associates. The Sunday-school teacher or Girls' Friendly Asso-
ciate who so indulges must not complain of
the pupil or member who follows her example. A visitor in a certain house was
amazed, on entering the parlor on Good
Friday evening, to find two whist tables in
operation, both occupied by church members
who had attended service in the morning.
The visitor was not surprised at the remark
of a Roman Catholic servant: "Well, they
don't think much of the day, whatever they
may pretend." And certainly the spectacle
was not an edifying one to those who made
no religious profession whatever. " All things

may be lawful for me, but all things are not expedient," and it is hard to see how anyone who desires to use this holy season as the Church intended it to be used can spend time and money on expensive amusements. Believe me, it is a bad symptom in the spiritual life when a Christian is thinking, not how much he can give up for his Lord, but how much he dares keep for himself.

Is. lviii.   1 Cor. x.

SECOND THURSDAY IN LENT.

IN THE SICK-ROOM.

"I AM an invalid," says some one; "I never go either to the theatre or opera; I never attend a party, or partake of any public amusement; hardly indeed, of any amusement at all.   How shall I keep Lent ?"

In the first place, so far as possible, get out of your world into God's world. I have been an invalid for months and years at a time, and I have seen a great deal of illness, so I am not speaking at random. The great temptation of a chronic invalid is to make the world centre in himself. The great in-

terests of mankind, and of the Church, charitable, and mission work, and Christian work
of every kind, are of no importance compared
to the position of a table or the serving of a
meal. We almost forget that these things
have any existence, or that we as individuals
have anything to do with them. I do not
mean to say that all chronic invalids are
irritable or selfish ; I must say frankly that I
have seen quite as much of these qualities in
nurses as in patients. But it is perfectly
natural—nay, it is unavoidable—when one is
shut up in a small space, to make that space
and its arrangements of great importance.
They *are* very important, and a kind and
faithful nurse will take care that no untidi-
ness or carelessness shall offend the eye ;
that the book or work or glass of drink shall
not be moved and set down just out of reach;
that the door shall not be left ajar to slam,
or the window to rattle. Such carelessness
is often nothing less than cruelty.

But making all allowances, I still say to
the invalid, get out of your little world into
the great world as often as possible. Recollect that you are still a member of Christ's
living body, and as such there must still be
some work for you to do. Especially at this

season, consider if there is not some way whereby you may help the Church in her great work of converting the world.

I would earnestly advise you to turn your attention to the subject of missions at home and abroad. If you are able to read, subscribe for the *Spirit of Missions* and read it all through. An excellent old Presbyterian lady once said that when she got her missionary paper she "just sat down and prayed right through it." Do you likewise, and at the same time consider how wonderful is this instrument of prayer, by which, in your chamber, you can reach the overworked man or woman toiling in China or Africa. You will soon find that your interest in the work grows as you learn more about it. You will find yourself looking out for news from particular stations and people, and thinking of Miss Wong and her orphans, and Miss Somebody Else and her Indians or Freedmen, as if they were personal friends.

Do not be content, however, with reading and praying. Try to do something. Many invalids are able to do more or less light work with their fingers, and find great comfort in it. Now at this time let your work be consecrated in a special manner. Lay

aside the fancy work, for something practical
and useful.   Let the drawn work give way
to the hospital towel, and the knitted lace
to the hospital sock.   Even if you can do
but little, let that little be done faithfully
and as regularly as possible, and the Lord of
the harvest will bless your gleanings as much
as the full sheaves of the stalwart reaper in
the field.

If you are earnest in watching for opportunities you may also practice self-denial in
other ways.   Are there no little luxuries
that you can do without, and so add a few
cents or dollars to your charity-purse ? Cannot the orange, or bunch of grapes, or bottle
of cologne be sent to some poor body who
keeps Lent all the year round ?   Is there no
service which you have been in the habit of
requiring from an attendant, and which, by a
little effort, you may perform for yourself ?
When a visitor comes in, can you not turn
the conversation from your own aches and
pains to something more pleasant and profitable ?   All these things are self-denials, and,
if used in the right spirit, will bring their
reward — a present reward in improved
cheerfulness, and so, often, in improved bodily
health ; a lasting reward in growth in grace,

and in that holiness which shall make you more fit for that world where there is no more any pain, because the former things are passed away.

Psalm lxxvii. Rev. vii. 9–17.

SECOND FRIDAY IN LENT.

THE USE OF FASTING.

WHAT is the use of fasting ?

The answer to this question is given in the collect which has formed the text of our meditations for the week. " That our flesh being subdued to the spirit, we may obey Thy godly motions in righteousness and true holiness.

The flesh, as the term is usually employed in Scripture, means the lower and earthly part of our nature. It is that part of us to which almost all the pleasures of sense address themselves. St. Paul tells us that they who are in the flesh—they who live for it alone—cannot please God (Rom. viii. 8) ; and he gives the reason, because they that are after the flesh do mind the things of the flesh,

The flesh, that is, as we have said, the lower part of our nature, has neither belief nor interest in anything but what can be seen and heard, and handled with hands. It cares for nothing but the things which belong to time, and must therefore perish with time. The invisible things which are eternal, and therefore the only real things, are as nothing to the man of the flesh, or at best but the idle dreams of enthusiasts. This being the case, it is easy to see why they who are in the flesh cannot please God.

Now this earthly and carnal nature, which is here called the flesh, remains in every one of us. We are all more or less under its influence. We are all prone to let the seen and temporal hide from our thoughts the unseen and eternal. The wants of the body are [imperative, and must be provided for, and with these needs are apt to come lusts. The lust of the flesh, the lust of the eye, and the pride of life are all intimately connected with real needs, and take on their names and faces.

Our bodies are useful servants, but bad and hard masters, and they are always striving to get the upper hand, and govern where they ought to obey. Therefore it is needful to rule them with a strong hand. St. Paul says, "I keep under my body, and bring it into subjection"; that is, literally, " I buffet it with blows, and treat it as a slave," and he gives us the reason for this conduct, "lest that by any means, when I have preached to others, I myself should be a castaway. (1 Cor. ix. 27.) The Scriptures, especially the Epistles, are full of warnings on this subject. "If ye live after the flesh, ye shall die : but if ye through the Spirit do mortify the deeds of the body ye shall live." (Rom. viii. 13.)

The flesh is to be subdued to the spirit ; to our own immortal spirit, and to the Holy Spirit. To our own spirit, because that is the part of us which is nearly related to God, capable of communion with Him, and even of being partaker of the Divine Nature (11 Pet. i. 4); to the Holy Spirit, because He is our Divine Guide and Comforter. The flesh is to be made thus subject, that it may know its place and be silent and quiet before its betters, that its voice may not hinder the voice of God. It must be taught to obey, that it may be the servant and not the master. And as soldiers are drilled in time of peace, when no enemy is at hand, that they

may be ready and skillful in time of war, so
our bodies may well be trained and brought
under discipline, that in the time of trial they
may be helps and not hindrances in running
the race which is set before us.

Is. xxxii.   1 Cor. ix.

SECOND SATURDAY IN LENT.

DANGERS AND MISTAKES.

THERE are two or three dangers and mistakes connected with this subject, which we
shall do well to consider.

The first is the danger of spiritual pride—
of considering our self-denials as good works,
whereby we acquire merit, and, so to speak,
bring God in debt to us. One would think,
at first sight, that no well-instructed Christian was in any such peril, yet a very slight
acquaintance with history will show the
painful absurdities which have grown out of
this idea, and the mischief and waste to which
it has led.

It is very hard for a man to take in the
idea that he cannot deserve anything of God
by his good works; that all his righteous-

nesses are as filthy rags, and that after his very best is done, he is but an unprofitable servant, doing no more than his duty; that he must accept salvation, if at all, as an absolutely free gift. His pride revolts at the idea. He does not like to feel that he is only a beggar. Hence the tendency, of which every faithful and experienced Christian is more or less conscious, to magnify his own good works, if not in the eyes of others, yet in his own secret soul. Pride is a subtle enemy, and never more to be dreaded than when it takes the form of that spiritual pride which apes humility. From this root have grown all sorts of noxious weeds; especially those exhibitions of self-torture which so revolt common sense in the lives of so-called saints—the pillar of Simon Stylites, the five orange seeds a day of Rose of Lima, and the like. Neither by precept nor example do the Scriptures countenance any such practices. On the contrary, our Lord's injunctions seem directed expressly against them. (S. Matt. vi. 16–18.)

Another danger to be guarded against is that of despising the body, as if it were of no account. The body is to be subject to the spirit, no doubt. It is a servant, and is to

4

be kept to a servant's place, even by severe discipline if need be, but it is to be kept in health and strength, that it may serve well its master. It is the tool of the spirit, and must be kept in good working order. He would be a foolish master who should so treat his tools or his servants as to disable them from work.

Our bodies are to be treated with respect because they are God's temples, in which it pleases Him to dwell. " Know ye not that your body is the temple of the Holy Ghost, which is in you ? " says the Apostle (1 Cor. vi. 19); and again, " Know ye not that ye are the Temple of God, and that the spirit of God dwelleth in you ?" and he adds, " If any man defile the temple of God, him will God destroy." (1 Cor. iii. 16.) From these considerations, it may be easily seen that those persons are guilty of sin who are willfully careless of the body; who for the sake of dress or amusement, or indulgence of any sort, injure their health and lessen their powers of usefulness.

Once more: The body is to be treated with respect because it has a share in our redemption. True, it is subject to decay and death. True, for a time it must molder in the dust, but it shall be raised again, and united to its kindred spirit, freed from all taint of sin and corruption. True, it is sown in dishonor and weakness, but it shall be raised in glory and power, to inherit immortality.

Job xiv.   1 Cor. iii.

SECOND SUNDAY IN LENT.

HELPLESSNESS AND HELP.

THE collect for this day is especially a prayer for help ; help for body and soul. The suppliant's plea is his helplessness. We have no power of ourselves to help ourselves, and so we turn to Him who is both able and willing to help us.

It is to be wished that Christians in general realized more fully their dependence upon God. We all go to Him for help in great matters—in deep afflictions, in strong temptations; but in the little things of every-day life, we forget or neglect to call upon Him; and it is in these very little things that we are defeated and overthrown by our ever-watchful enemy. "He that despiseth little things shall fall by little and little," said a wise man ; and no truer word was ever spoken. It is the small temptation which makes way for the great one. It is the mis-step which prepares for the fall.

Take an example : Theodore wakes in the morning feeling rather unwell and out of sorts. He has perhaps overslept when he wished to wake early, and is hurried in con-sequence. Proceeding to dress, he finds a button off, or a stud misplaced ; a real vex-ation, though a small one ; but Theodore never thinks of asking for help in such a matter as that. He would perhaps re-gard such a prayer as almost a mockery. The bell rings before he is ready, and he has, or thinks he has, no time for morning devotions. By the time he reaches his office, he is in a thoroughly bad humor, and ready to vent his annoyance on the first person who comes across him.

When Theodore reviews the events of the day, he is obliged to confess that he has made a sad failure. He sees, with shame, that he has been unjust and unkind ; that he has, perhaps, offended one of God's little ones, or put a stone of stumbling in the way of someone whom he is trying to influence for good. He confesses his sin with penitence and shame, but it does not occur to him to trace the trouble to its source—the failing to seek for help against the first temptation.

Oh that all of us, who profess and call ourselves Christians, could come to realize in our inmost souls, that in us, that is, in our flesh, dwells no good thing ; that in very deed we have no power of ourselves to help ourselves in great things or small ! It is a thought humbling to human pride, no doubt, but it is true. Every good thing, every good gift, is from above, and cometh down from the Father of lights (James i. 17), and thrives in the soil of this lower world only by careful cultivation. Spiritual strength, and the power to resist temptation, are no exception to this rule. They must come from above, in the first place, and they must be continually watered from above if they are to live. You might better set a willow-tree in the midst of the great American Desert, and expect it to grow there without irrigation, as to expect any Christian grace or virtue to live in your heart without constant watering from the Divine Fountain, which gave it life in the first place.

This fact of our utter helplessness to do

the least good thing of ourselves would be very discouraging ; would, indeed, lead us to utter despair if it stood alone. But God is all-knowing, and He sees that we have no power of ourselves to help ourselves. He is almighty. Nothing is too hard for Him. All things are in His hand, from the whole visible universe to the least grain which helps to make it ; from the highest arch- angel to the tiny baby which was christened yesterday, and whose christening robe was also its burial dress. Nothing is too great for His power, nothing too small for his care and love. He is our Father. He loves each one of His children as much as if that child were the only one, and He has laid up for each one such good things as pass man's understanding.

And this all-powerful, all-loving God knows all our needs and all our weakness. " He knoweth whereof we are made ; He re- membereth that we are but dust." (Ps. ciii. 14.) He sees that we have no power of our- selves to help ourselves, and His help is always ready. Yea, the whole power of Almighty God is enlisted on the side of the weakest child who is trying to please Him. But He will not force His help on any one.

His hand is always held out, but we are free to lay hold on it or not, as we will. We may neglect or slight His offers if we choose, but we must take the consequences. We may, if we please, kindle a fire for ourselves, and try to walk in the light of it ; but this shall we have of His hand : we shall lie down in sorrow. (Isa. l. 11.)

Isa. li.   S. John x. 19.

SECOND MONDAY IN LENT.

EVIL THOUGHTS AND THEIR REMEDY.

EVERY Christian knows what it is to be troubled with evil thoughts. Bunyan, than whom no uninspired man was ever better acquainted with the human heart, makes it one of his Pilgrim's trials that he bore away with him from the City of Destruction some of those things that he was conversant withal, especially his inward and carnal cogitations; and he adds, sorrowfully, " If I had my way, I would never think of those things more, but when I would do good, evil is present with me."

How often is his experience ours! How many times we find ourselves haunted with what we would fain forget! Some one offers us an affront. We have no desire to cherish a grudge, and perhaps we make an act of forgiveness on the spot ; but all day long the scornful word or the unkind act haunts our memory, and Satan conspires with the traitor in our own hearts to magnify the offense, and to suggest thoughts of malice and revenge. We are denied some pleasure or indulgence that others enjoy, and to which we think, perhaps, that we have a better right than they, and we dwell upon the matter, magnifying the forbidden pleasure or advantage till it becomes a dark fog, blotting out every pleasant prospect and shutting us up in measureless discontent.

I believe that invalids are particularly subject to this kind of temptation. The horizon of the sick person is narrow at the best, and a small cloud suffices to obscure it. Moreover, there are certain disorders which seem of themselves particularly favorable to evil thoughts. The patient is, or fancies himself, neglected or forgotten. He is tempted to envy those better off than himself. He thinks of all the good work he has done, and of all he might do, and he is tempted to think hardly of the Master, who seems to have rejected his service. These and still darker thoughts beset the daily couch and nightly pillow of the invalid, till he feels as if Satan in bodily presence were standing at his bedside.

Now what is the remedy for this unhappy state of things ? The first thing to be done is to recognize these thoughts as sins. We are too apt to excuse them to ourselves as mere infirmities, consequent on our state of health. They may be so to some extent. All our sins are the consequence of some temptation. So long as we constantly make excuses for our faults, so long they will stay by us, and consider themselves as welcome guests. Let us call them by their right names to begin with, and, like the malicious dwarf in the fairy tale, they are half conquered already.

The next thing to be done with our evil thoughts is to crowd them out. It has been said that Nature abhors a vacuum, but Satan loves one because it gives him a place wherein to bestow his wares. Let us try to so occupy our mind with good things that there shall be no room for the bad ones.

Let us fill our memories with good and pleasant things, that we may from time to time take out our treasures, and refresh ourselves with the sight of them.   Christian found his inward enemies were vanquished when he looked upon his broidered coat— that robe of Christ's righteousness given him instead of his own rags ; when he read in his roll—that evidence of his salvation given to every humble believer in God's word ; and above all, when his thoughts waxed warm about the place to which he was going. Try his method.

Then, too, we must use the weapon put into our hands for this very purpose—the sword of the Spirit, which is the Word of God ; and to the end that we may have the full benefit thereof, we must accustom ourselves to its use.   We must store our memory with its promises,its counsels and instructions.   I once asked a venerable minister what book I should read in Lent.   His answer was, " The Bible"; and he added, "I could wish that Christians would put aside all other books during Lent, and read the Bible alone."   Without going so far as this, I would earnestly warn every one not to let the Bible be crowded out by any book, however edifying. Do not be content with merely reading, but study it. Learn by heart such passages as are likely to be most useful, and so familiarize yourself with the book as to be able to turn at once to any-thing you want. A sick bed or chamber is not the best place to begin this practice, but it is better begun there than never.

Above all, let us, like Christian in the shadow of death, betake ourselves to the weapon called "all-prayer." Let us make haste to escape to Him who is our strong tower and house of defense. Let the lan-guage of our hearts be that of the Psalmist : "Into thy hands I commend my spirit, for Thou hast redeemed me, O Lord, thou God of truth." (Ps. xxxi. 5.) So shall He de-fend us under His wings and we shall be safe under His feathers ; His faithfulness and truth shall be our shield and buckler. (Ps. xci. 4.)

    Ps. xxxv.   St. John xiv.

SECOND TUESDAY IN LENT.

MEDITATION.

THE best remedies for evil thoughts are good thoughts.

It is, I fear, a sorrowful truth that in these days of activity and bustle, in the Church and out of it, the duty and privilege of Christian meditation is in danger of being pushed into the background, or forgotten altogether. We read a few verses in the Bible, morning and evening. Perhaps we keep some religious book on our table, and read a little every day. All this is very well as far as it goes. But how many Christians ever sit down to think out anything for themselves? We may "hear and read" the Bible, but unless we " mark, learn, and inwardly digest " as well, our souls may be half-starved in presence of a royal banquet.

Meditation, that is to say, serious and connected thought on a given subject, is not an easy task. But, as an excellent writer aptly asks, " Who ever said any Christian duty was easy?" Meditation is always hard at first. It is often difficult to those who have practiced it for years : there is so much to be done, and so little time; there are so many trials of temper and feeling in our daily life, whether that life be passed out of doors or in the confinement of a sick-room.

This is all true. And every one of these statements is a plea for the practice I am advocating. There are so many distractions, that we all need the quiet of that "little sanctuary" which God has promised to be to His people in all lands. (Ezek. xi. 16.) There are so many trials of temper and feeling, that we all need to claim the promise, "Thou shalt hide them privily by Thy presence from the provoking of all men." (Ps. xxxi. 20.) There is so much to be done, and so little time to do it in, that we cannot afford to miss any help which our Master has put in our way. As well might the tree planted by the river (Jer. xvii. 8) spend all its strength in putting forth branches and leaves, and forget to stretch out its roots to the pure cold waters which run at its foot. Unless it does so stretch out its roots, it might as well grow like the heath in the desert.

"But I do not know where to begin,"

says some one ; " I do not know what to
think about." This is surely a needless
difficulty. Is not the deep, unfailing well at
hand, yea, under your hand ? Have you no
Bible ? Let us look for a moment at that
priceless model of meditation, the cxix.
Psalm. What is the key-note of that psalm
but the consideration of God's Word? " I
will meditate in Thy statutes." "Open mine
eyes, that I may behold the wondrous things
of Thy law." "Teach me, O Lord, the
way of Thy statutes." And so on from
beginning to end. It is the Word of God
which must be the text of our meditations.

" But how shall I set about it ?

You are perhaps a Sunday-school teacher
or pupil. (You should, if possible, be one or
the other.) If so, you have the subject of
your meditation cut out for you in your next
Sunday's lesson. I advise you to begin by
memorizing it. In that way you can carry
it about with you wherever you go. Then
turn it over in your mind, verse by verse, yea,
word by word. Sift it as if you were hunt-
ing for diamonds. Say to yourself, "Do I
understand the exact meaning of this word,
or that allusion ? How shall I explain that

point ? How shall I frame a question which shall make the pupil bring out the meaning for himself?" And finally, "What does the lesson teach me?" For, be assured, unless it does say something to you, you will never make it speak to any one else. If there were more of this kind of preparation, the superintendent would not so often be grieved by the sorrowful spectacle of a teacher sitting idly before an idle class, because he or she "has finished the lesson, and does not know what to say."

Permit me to give a short example to illustrate my meaning. Take the first verse of the second chapter of St. Matthew—a simple passage, and very familiar. " Jesus was born in Bethlehem." Where is Bethlehem ? What do I know about its situation, its distance from Jerusalem, its history and present condition ? Was it the home of Jesus' parents ? How did He happen to be born there ? Then come the momentous questions : Who was this babe of Bethlehem ? Why was He born ? What is He to me ? And so you see, this simple historical verse lifts for you the veil of the Holy of Holies, where you can but wonder and adore. The prayer-book, also, will furnish abundant subjects for thought.   Take the collect for the day; say, for example, the ninth Sunday after Trinity, which has a direct bearing on this subject. Why is it so important to have right thoughts? What is the relation between thinking and doing?   What passages of Scripture bearing on this point can I remember?   And so on through the whole collect. There is, perhaps, not a prayer in the Church service which will not afford matter for a week's meditation ; and no one knows the wealth concealed in the prayer-book who has not treated it in this way.   Try it, and see if at the end of the Lenten season the Church service does not say more to you than ever it did before.

Ps. cxix. 1–24.   II Peter 1.

NOTE.—The substance of this and the next chapter was printed in *Church Work*, some time ago.

THIRD WEDNESDAY IN LENT.

MEDITATION.

"MEDITATION is all very well for people of leisure," says some one, "but I am busy from morning till night.   I have no time."

To this I answer: "Are you quite sure you have no time? Let me ask you to look back upon your day, and tell yourself honestly how much time has been spent in melancholy musing, in useless regret, or worse than useless foreboding; perhaps, in brooding over some real or fancied injury or affront. Surely these hours would have been more pleasantly and profitably spent in the way I have suggested. Just because you have so much to do, you need the refreshment of the hidden spring—of the pure water which flows from the Fountain of Life."

"I am engaged in a great deal of Church and charitable work," says another; "has it not been said that labor is prayer? and may it not take the place of meditation as well?"

Just as well, and no better. You might as well say that labor is eating. It is a pretty and plausible saying, but it is not true. Labor is *not* prayer, any more than it is food or sleep. No one needs more the refreshment of the hidden spring than the person who is engaged in mission or charitable work. There is so much to discourage and dishearten, there are so many failures and disappointments and mistakes, that the worker

5

needs all the aid and comfort procurable not to grow morbid and discouraged.

" Yes, it is all very well for healthy people," says another, " but I am an invalid." Just because you are an invalid do you need to learn the art of governing your thoughts. No one is tempted more than an invalid to the indulgence of those useless and harmful musings of which I have spoken. Sharp and severe illness is an occupation in itself. But to the chronic patient, able to be about a little, perhaps to do a little light work, how long are the hours of the day! how much longer those of the night! How fancy pictures to us the pleasures of the world which we cannot enjoy! How often do Satan and our own corrupt hearts conspire to suggest hard and unkind thoughts of friends and attendants, yea, even of God Himself. How are our uneasy pillows haunted with the ghosts of dead joys and hopes and plans, and still more dread phantoms of sins and failures and fears for the future! I have been a bad sleeper all my life, and in many an hour of wakefulness have I blessed the old-fashioned Sunday-school method of " seven verses and a hymn," which stored my mind with whole chapters of the Bible, and with the best devotional poetry. I wish this old fashion could become a new fashion again. I have never seen a better.

" But there is such an abundance of good books !"

True, but all the books in the world are worth very little to the person who is content with merely reading them. We can think, moreover, when we cannot read, and half an hour's earnest and prayerful consideration of a chapter or verse of God's word will be of more value than a dozen commentaries without such consideration.

It is good always to begin and end our meditations with prayer. It is good, too, at times, to turn our meditation into contemplation ; in simply making real to ourselves His presence who has said, " Lo, I am with you always." (St. Matt. xxviii. 20.) " If any man open the door, I will come in and sup with him, and he with Me." (Rev. iii. 20.)

Let me beg of all who read this chapter and who have never done so, to make trial of its recommendations through the Lenten season. Do not be discouraged, though you fail many times, though again and again you find your thoughts wandering to the ends of the earth. Drive them back to their ap-

pointed work every time. By and by you
will find them less inclined to stray. The
hard task will become a pleasure, and you
will be amply rewarded for your pains when
you find Divine truth growing more and
more clear and precious, when you find yourself better and better able to turn away from
painful and unprofitable thoughts, to take
refuge in the Lord's presence from the provoking of all men, and to rest under the
shadow of the Great Rock in the weary land.
Then your heart shall not be " like the heath
in the desert, and shall not see when good
cometh," but rather "as a tree planted by the
waters, and that spreadeth out her roots by
the river ; and shall not see when heat cometh, but her leaf shall be green ; and shall
not be careful in the year of drought, neither
shall cease from yielding fruit." (Jer. xvii. 6, 8.)

Jer. xvii.   Rev. iii.

THIRD THURSDAY IN LENT.

PRAYER.

THE Christian is to pray without ceasing; that is, he is always to be in the spirit of prayer. He is, by God's help, to strive to keep himself in such a state that he can at any moment lift up his heart and mind to his Heavenly Father, and that as much in the round of his daily business as in his closet. He is to strive to carry about with him an habitual sense of the presence of God, and of dependence upon Him for all things.

" Use lessens marvel," says the old proverb, and the saying is true. The most surprising discoveries in science, the most wonderful applications of these discoveries to the arts, cease to astonish us in a very short time. There is nothing in the Arabian Nights which sounds more incredible than that the movement of a wheel turned by a water-fall should light up a great city. Yet every child has become used to the electric light, and

thinks no more marvel of it than his grand-
father did of a candle.

So it is with prayer. Every child of a
Christian mother is taught to pray as soon as
it can speak, and accepts without question
the instruction that prayer is talking to his
Father in Heaven. He prays God to bless
his father, who is sailing on the sea, and his
brother in a distant city, and it seems no
more wonderful to him than that the street
light should make a pretty picture on the
wall of his nursery. And yet what a wonder
is prayer, when we come to consider it! All
the marvels of man's discovery and inven-
tion shrink into nothing before it. I was
once telling some little girls about the tele-
phone and saying how strange it seemed to
talk with a friend twenty miles away.
"Yes," said one, "but we can talk to God
without a wire."

The great God who upholds the Universe
in His hand, and orders all things by His
omnipotent power and wisdom, has his ear
always open to the appeal of his feeblest
child. Not a sigh from a sick-bed, not a
prayer lisped at the mother's knee, not a cry
from the deepest dungeon, but is heard and
marked by Him. From every place on earth,

the way is open to His throne. The mother who has a son in China can send him help by this road. The poor widow in the alms-house can lighten the trials of her lot; yea, though she have not a penny to give to the cause, she can help the missionary in the farthest distant field by her prayers. When we can do no more for our friends, we can commend them to the prayers of the Church. Alas ! we too often wait till we can do no more.

I close this chapter with an extract from Professor Phelps's admirable book, " The Still Hour."

" In the vestibule of St. Peter's at Rome is a doorway which is walled up, and marked with a cross. It is opened but four times in a century. On Christmas eve, once in twenty-five years, the Pope approaches it in princely state, with a retinue of cardinals in attend-ance, and begins the demolition of the door by striking it three times with a silver ham-mer. When the passage is opened, the mul-titude pass into the nave of the cathedral and up to the altar by an avenue which the majority of them never entered before, and never will enter thus again.

" Imagine that the way to the Throne of

Grace were like the Porta Santa, inaccessible save once in a quarter of a century, on the twenty-fifth of December, and then only with august solemnities, conducted by great dignitaries in a distant city. Conceive that it were now ten years since you or I, or any other sinner, had been *permitted* to pray; and that fifteen long years must drag themselves away before we could venture to approach God; and that, at the most, we could not hope to pray more than two or three times in a life-time—with what solicitude should we wait for the coming of that holy day !

"We should lay our plans of life, select our homes, build our houses, choose our professions, with reference to a pilgrimage in that twenty-fifth year. We should reckon time by the opening of that sacred door as by epochs. No other one thought would engross so much of our lives, or kindle our sensibilities so exquisitely, as the thought of prayer. It would be of more significance to us than the thought of death is now. Fear would grow to horror at the thought of dying before that Jubilee.

" Yet on that great day, amidst an innumerable throng, within sight and hearing of

stately rites, what would prayer be to us?
Who would value it in the comparison of
those still moments, that

'Sacred silence of the mind,'

in which we can now find God every day and
everywhere? That day would be more like
the day of Judgment to us than like the
sweet minutes of converse with our Father,
which we may now have every hour. We
should appreciate this privilege of hourly
prayer if it were once taken from us."
Ps. lxxvii.   St. Luke xi. 1-14.

THIRD FRIDAY IN LENT.

PRAYER

WHAT is prayer?
Prayer, in its primary sense, means simply
asking. We find the word constantly used
in this sense in Scripture and elsewhere; as
when Elijah says to the widow woman of
Zarephath, "Fetch me, I pray thee, a little
water." But prayer, as the word has come
to be used in the whole Church, has a much
higher signification. It means speaking to

God. It means pouring out our hearts to
Him—telling Him all our wants, our wishes,
our hindrances and temptations, our trials
from without and from within. It means
asking not only for ourselves, but for others;
our families, our fellow church-members, our
pupils, our country and its rulers, yea, even
our enemies. (S. Matt. v. 44.) There is no
matter too great for it, and none too small.
There is no man so holy as not to need it to
keep him good, and none so wicked that he
may not use it to make him better. The
way of prayer is open to every one. It is the
open door set before every child of God, which
no man can shut. The Christian may be a
slave, or a prisoner watched by soldiers, beset
by spies, loaded with fetters in the deepest
dungeon on earth. In the prisons of the
Inquisition, the captive was condemned to
perpetual silence. Not a word, not a groan,
must escape his lips, on pain of the gag. But
his cruel and relentless jailers could not prevent him from speaking to his God, nor could
they prevent the unspoken words from entering the ear for which they were intended.
That was beyond their power.

The courts of earthly kings are places of
resort for great people, for the noble, the

rich and beautiful of their subjects. The poor and lowly have no room there. But the courts of the King of kings are as free to the poorest laboring man and woman as to those to whose luxury they minister; nay, it may well be that the slave will find entrance and kind entertainment when his master is shut out. Nor is ignorance or weakness of intellect a bar to acceptance. The broken language of the poor negro, the lisping accents of the little child, are as musical to the great Father of all as the hymns of the poet, or the highest flights of the philosopher. He sees the heart, and it is the heart which prays.

What is requisite to acceptable prayer ?

First of all, faith. "He that cometh to God, must believe that He is, and that He is a rewarder of them that diligently seek Him." (Heb. xi. 6.) A moment's consideration makes this perfectly plain. We shall not ask of any person a boon, unless we believe that the person exists, and that we shall gain something by the application. We must ask in faith; that is, in the belief that we are speaking to a kind Father, whose heart is warm toward us, and who loves to do us good.

Some good people believe that God will

give us just what we ask for. They will even
tell us that, if we do not so receive, it is because we do not ask in faith.   I believe this
to be a mischievous mistake.   God knows
our necessities before we ask, and He also
knows our ignorance in asking.   We do not
always know whether the thing we ask is
the best thing.   Our Father sees our lives
" in the whole of our duration, whether now
or ever so many ages hence," as a distinguished author has it, and

"The All-wise is the All-loving too!"

All things are in his power, and it costs Him
no more to give one than another.   Every
prayer reaches His ear and heart, and every
one is answered, but not always in the way
we expect.   Sometimes He gives us something else than the thing we desire, as a tender mother gives her child wholesome food at
the same time that she withholds the coveted
but unwholesome dainty.   Sometimes, too,
like the same wise mother, He answers, gently
but firmly, *No!*   But even when He says
No, He does not leave His child uncomforted.
"I have learned by experience," says an
aged saint of God, "that when He refuses
me anything, by and by He comforts me in
Himself without it."

We must pray with faith, and with resigna-
tion to God's will, but we must also ask with
perseverance. Our Lord gives us the war-
rant for this in the parables of the importu-
nate friend (St. Luke xi), and of the unjust
judge (St. Luke xviii). We are to "pray
always, and not to faint." (St. Luke xviii. 1.)
We are to " pray always, with all prayer and
supplication." (Eph. vi. 18.) We are to " pray
without ceasing." (1 Thess. v. 17.) We must
not be content with asking once or twice,
but we must keep asking again and again.
Some blessing will come in answer to perse-
vering prayer, though it may not always be
the one we seek.

There is one blessing, and that the greatest, which we may always ask in full confidence of receiving, and that is the gift of the
Holy Spirit. Our Lord tells us that earthly
parents are not so ready to give good
gifts to their children, as His father and ours
is to give the Holy Spirit to them that ask
Him. (St. Luke xi. 13.) And this very gift
helps us to pray acceptably, for "the Spirit
also helpeth our infirmities," interceding for
us with "groanings which cannot be uttered."
"And He that searcheth the heart knoweth
what is the mind of the Spirit, because He

maketh intercession for the saints, according
to the will of God." (Rom. viii. 26, 27.)

Ps. xxv.   St. Luke xi. 1–14.

THIRD SATURDAY IN LENT.

INTERCESSION.

WE are not to be selfish in our prayers.
Our Lord teaches us this lesson in the very
first words of the form of prayer which He
Himself has given us: " When ye pray, say,
Our Father."

Of course, if God is *our* Father, He is *your*
Father and *mine* as well.   Nay, we must lay
hold of this truth of God's individual care
and love for His children, before we can pray
as we ought.   But our Lord would bring
home to our minds that, as we are members
of Christ, so we are members one of another.
We are sons and daughters of the great
King, and so brothers and sisters ; and
thence it follows that, as members of one
family, we have duties to perform toward each
other.   It is the very definition of a member
that it is part of an organism fitted to perform certain offices for the good of the whole.
We see, in the human body, that the hand

has one office, the eye another, and so on. So it is in the body of Christ, which is His Church—each member has his place and his duties. One of these duties is intercessory prayer.

We have the commands of God in Holy Scripture for this matter, which should of itself be enough for us: " I exhort, therefore, that first of all supplications, prayers, intercessions, and giving of thanks be made for all men. For this is good and acceptable in the sight of God our Saviour." (1 Tim. ii. 1, 3.) St. Paul again and again asks the prayers of those to whom his letters are addressed. " Brethren, pray for us." (1 Thess. v. 25.) " Continue in prayer, and watch in the same with thanksgiving; withal praying also for us " (Col. iv. 2, 3); and so in other places. Our Lord Himself, our perfect pattern, sets us the highest example of this kind of prayer, concluding His last discourse to the twelve with that most wonderful intercession contained in the seventeenth chapter of St. John.

Following the example of her Head, the Church teaches us the same lesson. We are taught to pray for our rulers, for the clergy, for all sorts and conditions of men.

The Litany is in a great measure made up of intercessions. Also in the most solemn service of all—that of the Holy Communion—we are taught to pray for the whole estate of Christ's church militant.

These reasons ought to be enough, if there were no others, to move us to the duty of intercession. It hardly seems, indeed, as if we ought to need a *command*, however glad we may be of the encouragement. Is it not a privilege as well as a duty to carry our friends' dangers and needs and trials to the Mercy Seat ? Is it not much to commend to our Father's care our nearest and dearest, and to join our prayers to theirs, thus obtaining the benefit of the promise that when two are agreed on earth as touching anything they shall ask, it shall be done for them ? (St. Matt. xviii. 19.)

We may help those by our prayers whom we can help in no other way. The most obstinate sinner, the most rampant infidel, the most careless and indifferent person in the world, cannot keep his friends from praying for him. The son may disregard his mother's tears and counsels, but her prayers will follow him in spite of himself. Nay, more, the very consciousness that such prayers were following him has kept more than one such wanderer from an irretrievable fall, and brought him back to his mother's arms. Prayer girdles the earth more quickly than the electric spark, and no one upon that earth is out of its reach.

Those who can help the good works of the Church in no other way can do so by prayer. The invalid in her room or on her bed, who is too weak perhaps to hold a pen or a needle, can help the toiler in China or the far West; can call down blessing from the Divine Treasury, and strength and grace from the Fountain of all good, for the man or woman she has never seen. The poor old black woman in the gallery of the church, without a penny to call her own, can strengthen the hands and cheer the heart of the eloquent missionary bishop who enters the pulpit to make known to the people what God has wrought in a distant land. Surely such a privilege is worth a great deal to the true child of God, who desires with the whole heart the coming of her Lord and His kingdom, but yet can do nothing, humanly speaking, to hasten it on.

It is certain that we cannot honestly pray for people without wishing to help them in

6

other ways. The man whose prayers are a
mere decent form, or a sheer pretence and
hypocrisy, may pray in general for the cause
of Christ in the world without raising his
hand or denying himself one indulgence for
it, but not the man who prays in earnest,
" Thy kingdom come, Thy will be done on
earth as it is in heaven." To him, " Thy
kingdom come " means also, " Let me help
to bring it," and " Thy will be done " means
also, " Let me do it." It is said of St. Chry-
sostom, that he kept a box on the stool
where he was wont to kneel in prayer, and
with every petition for the poor he deposited
a coin in the treasury.

Finally, praying for others helps us to
pray for ourselves. When our hearts seem
dull and cold, and so heavy that we cannot
raise them up to heaven, an intercession will
often lend them wings. We shall go back
to our own needs with renewed faith and
hope, and find the burden removed that held
us down.

Let us, then, be instant in prayer and supplication, not only for ourselves, but for our
friends and relatives, our pupils or teachers,
for our own parish and all its interests, for
the Church at large, for our country, and for

all sorts and conditions of men. And let us not be weary in so doing, till "they shall teach no more every man his neighbor, and every man his brother, saying, Know the Lord ; for all shall know Him, from the least of them even unto the greatest of them." (Jer. xxxi. 34.) Yea, " the knowledge of the Lord shall cover the earth as the waters cover the sea." (Hab. ii. 14.)

Is. lxii.   1 Tim. ii.

THIRD SUNDAY IN LENT.

OUR ENEMIES.

IN the collect for the day we ask for defense against our enemies. "Stretch out Thy right hand to be our defense against our enemies." The right hand is the symbol both of power and skill. It is especially so among Orientals, with whom it is reserved for all the nobler offices, the left hand performing those which are more humble or unclean. We find in the Psalms and the prophets, that the right hand of God is usually spoken of as the especial seat of His power, as in Ps. cxviii. 16. " The right hand of the Lord hath the pre-eminence; the right hand of the Lord bringeth mighty things to pass."

To the Christian the right hand of the Lord means even more than it did to the Jew, for it is there that his Saviour is enthroned, and ever remains, to make intercession for him. Saint Stephen was vouchsafed the vision of his risen Lord, thus placed, no doubt, to strengthen him for his coming trial, and there shall we all see him who are counted worthy to attain to the first resurrection. " To think," said an aged saint to whom I had just been reading the Bible, "to think that I shall see Jesus at the right hand of God ! Oh, if I might but once touch His hand !" The very thought lighted up her plain face with a smile which made it beautiful.

God is our defense. All the Scriptures are full of the thought, but especially the Psalms. God will help the poor and needy, and will set him at rest. (Ps. lxii. 6.) " The Lord is my stony rock and my defense, my Saviour, my God and my might, in whom I will trust ; my buckler, the horn also of my salvation, and my refuge." (Ps. xviii. 2.) " Though I walk through the valley of the shadow of death, I will fear no evil ; for Thou art with me ; Thy rod and Thy staff comfort me." (Ps. xxiii. 4.)

And so again and again we have our
Heavenly Father's promise to defend His
children against all their enemies, both
spiritual and temporal. True, we must walk
through the wilderness of this world, but we
need not walk alone. True, we walk in the
midst of enemies, yet "they that be with us
are more than they that be with them" (2
Kings vi. 16), and if our eyes were opened,
like those of the prophet's servant, we should,
like him, see the angel hosts sent for defense.
We may, nay we must, hunger and thirst, but
the Lord will cause waters to break out in
the wilderness, and streams in the desert.
(Isa. xxxv. 6.) We need be afraid of
none of its terrors. The light will break
forth and the sun will rise, and show the
ground covered with manna for our refreshment.

The thought of our God as a defense and
shield should be a help and comfort to those
Christians who are troubled with fears.
There are those, especially among invalids,
whose lives are made a burden to themselves
and others by needless fears. They are afraid
of lightning, of fire, of robbers, of they know
not what. They feel as if every thunderbolt
had a special commission for them ; as if

every blast of wind were a destroying angel.
These fears are often merely nervous symptoms, but even then they are very much
under the control of the patient. Let me
say to such an one, Do but think, do but try to
realize to yourself the fact that the Lord's
right hand is stretched out to be your defense in all dangers—that He will defend
thee under His wings, and thou shalt be safe
under His feathers. Consider that the darkness is no darkness to Him, but the night is
as clear as the day. (Ps. cxxxix. 11.)

> " When first before the mercy-seat
> Thou didst thine all to Him commit,
> He gave thee warrant from that hour
> To trust His mercy, love, and power."

Are not these terrors, then, an affront to
Him, as implying a distrust in His plighted
word ? Dismiss them, then ! Send them
back to the darkness where they belong, and
let your motto be, "I will lay me down in
peace, and take my rest, for it is Thou, Lord,
that makest time to dwell in safety." (Ps.
iv. 8)

Ps. xci.   St. John xiv.

THIRD MONDAY IN LENT.

OUR ENEMIES.

WE have seen that the collect we are considering has its foundation, like all the prayers that we learn at the knee of our mother, the Church, in the promises of God's word, and are therefore sure to be answered in some way. Observe, however, that it is nowhere said in the Bible that we are not to meet with adversities. Nay, we are told the express contrary. All His life long our Master endured hardship and trouble; and the servant is not above his Master. "In the world ye shall have tribulation," says our Lord to His apostles, but He graciously adds: "Be of good cheer, I have overcome the world." (St. John xvi. 33.)

What are those enemies which the Christian has to dread, and against which he has special need to pray for deliverance?

Here, again, our Lord leaves us in no doubt. "Fear not them which kill the body, and are not able to kill the soul" (St. Matt. x.

28); and again, " Fear not them that kill the body, and, after that, have no more that they can do." (St. Luke xii. 4.) This shuts out all that class of terrors of which I spoke in the last chapter. The cruelest murderer, the most destructive storm or earthquake, the most noisome pestilence, can only kill that which must die at any rate—which brought its death-warrant with it when it came into the world. They cannot destroy the real man or woman ; nay, all their forces combined cannot deprive him of the very least of those things which God hath prepared for them that love Him (1 Cor. ii. 9); nor of one moment of that eternal life which God hath given us in His Son. (1 John v. 11.)

Clearly, then, the enemies we have to fear are those which assault and hurt the soul, and which, unless steadfastly resisted, are able to make our way dark and perilous, if not to deprive us of that inheritance which has been prepared for us. It is they whom we are to combat with all our force, and against whom we must specially ask our great Defender to stretch out His right hand. Yet even here we must not show ourselves coward and craven. We are soldiers of Christ. Let us never forget that. Every battle is fought for Him, every victory is a victory over His enemies as well as our own. He will never leave us to struggle alone, but is always with us, though we cannot always perceive Him. Let us, then, be strong in the Lord, and in the power of His might, knowing that His Father, who gave us to Him, is greater than all, and none is able to pluck us out of His hand. (St. John x. 29.)

Our spiritual enemies may all be classed under three heads—the world, the flesh, and the devil. Against these we are to fight manfully and to the death, never laying down our arms, never relaxing our vigilance, and, even though apparently beaten for the time, never giving up, till our Great Commander shall see our warfare accomplished, and call us home. It is the Christian's paradox that there is no peace except in war. If we give up the contest, we become slaves; and though our conquerors give us all the goods they have to bestow in this life, they do but treat us as cannibals treat their prisoners—fattening them, that they may devour them at last.

Hab. ii. St. Luke xii.

THIRD TUESDAY IN LENT.

THE WORLD.

EVERY general strives to know all that he can about his enemy, his nature and position, his powers and resources, and tries to foresee the plans of that enemy's attack, that he may be able to meet and frustrate them. Let us, then, inquire a little into the nature of those foes which beset our homeward path, and which would, if they could, hinder us from reaching the rest prepared for us in our Father's house. First of all, what is meant by the world ?

The world means all that outside of ourselves which is alienated from and opposed to God, which is governed by and devoted to the things which are temporal, and ignores, if it does not hate, the things which are eternal. It is very wise in its own eyes ; yea, according to its own canons, and from its own standpoint, wiser than the children of light. It is dreadfully in earnest in the things which it pursues, though those things may be of the most frivolous description. It gets into all sorts of places, alas even into the Church itself, running here and there for meat, and grudging if it be not satisfied, which, indeed, it never is. It is a severe master to its votaries, exacting the hardest and the most exclusive services and the most cruel sacrifices, and rewarding them at last with husks and rags.

The world puts on many disguises. To one it comes under the name of business, demanding of its slave that he shall give up everything else for the pursuit of money. It does not make this demand of every man at the beginning, and in so many words. No, it is more cunning than that. It tells him that it is his duty to provide for his family, not only needful food and clothes and the means of education, but a fine house in a fashionable quarter, and as many luxuries as his neighbor possesses. It makes him press hard on those who labor for him, and exact much work for little pay. It makes him rent tenements to men and women which are not fit for pigs to live in, and grudge the smallest outlay for the health and comfort of his tenants. It makes him plan and scheme to add a few thousands more to his useless millions, by raising the price of fuel and food to the poor man. By and by, the world has done with him. He speculates a little too rashly, and his wealth goes as it came. Or God says to him, " Thou fool ! This night thy soul shall be required of thee ! " and he goes forth from the visible and unreal to the invisible and real, a shivering, hungry, naked soul, homeless to all eternity. And that world for which he has toiled and sacrificed misses him as much as he missed the consumptive girl who breathed the foul air of his factory till her young life was poisoned, and she dropped at her machine, and went home to die.

The world comes to a woman with a family of little ones, and bids her leave these immortal pledges of God's love to servants, to learn their very prayers from alien lips, and spend her nights in amusements, and her days in planning for the nights. It exacts of her that she shall risk her health and blunt her sense of delicacy by immodest and insufficient clothing. It tell her that these things are necessary, a debt that she owes to society, and whispers that she can make up for all that needs an atonement, by putting on a sober dress and going to church regularly in Lent, or by giving about the fiftieth part of what her dress costs in charity.

To another woman, the world comes in sober attire, with a housewifely apron and a bunch of keys. It has another bait for this one, who would not attend a ballet for the world, and looks with horror on a game of cards. This woman's world is her house-keeping, and she can see nothing else. She would feel herself disgraced forever, if her neighbor put up more cans of fruit or gave more kinds of cake to her company than her-self. Talk to her of the sewing-school or the district visiting society, and she will tell you of her anxieties about the doing up of her lace curtains. Tell her of the needs of the heathen, at home or abroad, she may listen politely, but her duty, she says, is to her own family, and she cannot do anything to help you because her dining-room chairs are quite out of fashion, and she must have new ones. Ask her to see that her little daughter has her catechism learned for Sunday-school, and she will tell you, as she sews the elaborate and costly trimming on the child's dress, that she has no time.

We are in bondage to the world so soon as we let the seen and temporal, no matter

in what shape it comes, blind us to the unseen and eternal. We are in cruel bondage
when we let the fear of what the world may
say about us lead us to do what we know to
be inconsistent with our baptismal vows and
our loyalty to our Lord. We are slaves to
the world when we allow any of the things
which live in time and perish with time to
possess our hearts to the exclusion of those
things which belong to eternity. It is true,
that as long as we are on the earth, the
things of earth must claim much of our attention. Thank God! all these things may
be made holy by an honest intention. But
we cannot serve God and mammon, and he
who tries to do so will in the end find himself deserted of both, and left to himself, that
worst of all fates, from which may God in
His mercy keep us all!

Psalm lxxiii.   St. Luke xvi.

FOURTH WEDNESDAY IN LENT.

THE FLESH.

WHO and what are the enemies that come to us under this name?

All those pleasures and pursuits which appeal only or chiefly to our senses; to our earthly and mortal natures; to that carnal mind which St. Paul tells us is not, and by its very nature cannot be, subject to the law of God. The enemies of the flesh are all the more dangerous because they appear under the disguise of friends—of things harmless, and even necessary, in themselves. They are like slaves, serving their masters in deed, but with secret enmity, always watching their chance to rebel, and the cruelest of tyrants when they gain the mastery. Just because we cannot do without them, we need to guard against their abuse.

How much money is wasted every year upon table luxuries, which the consumers would be as well or better without! How

many become such slaves to certain articles
of food and drink that they find it almost
impossible to do without these things, though
they know, on the best authority, that health
is being injured by their use! How many
are vexed and put out of temper if their bodily comfort is invaded in the smallest degree!
More than once have I seen the comfort of
a whole table-full destroyed, and the meal
rendered distasteful, by some one person,
who persisted in finding fault with everything set upon the board.

It may seem at first sight a singular statement, that invalids need especially to maintain a strict watch over themselves in the
matter of indulgence in eating and drinking,
but I believe it is true. There is perhaps
more excuse to be made for them than for
most others, because they are, perforce,
obliged to think a good deal of the matter;
but for this very reason they need to guard
themselves against dwelling too much on it,
and against harmful self-indulgence. I have
seen invalids keep themselves in a chronic
state of discomfort, and consequent fretful-
ness, by eating too much. And it is an odd
circumstance, though one well known to
doctors and nurses, that these very people

àre often fully convinced that they eat little or nothing.

Invalids are often led to injure themselves by an inordinate use of the drugs and stimulants prescribed by physicians. They find the use of such remedies followed by pleasant sensations, and take them many times when they are not really needful; and so are made the opium drunkard, the chloral drunkard, and not infrequently the whisky drunkard as well. I use the word advisedly. The man who lives upon laudanum, the woman who indulges in morphine or chloral, is just as much a drunkard as the man or woman who gets tipsy in the corner saloon, and usually an even more hopeless case. The whisky drunkard will often admit that he is such; the opium drunkard never.

The remedy for all these evils is to be found in one word — temperance. "Every man that striveth for the mastery is temperate in all things." (1 Cor. ix. 25.) The word "temperance" has come to be used in such a confined sense, that we are in danger of forgetting its larger application. We are to be temperate in all things; that is, we are to use them in such moderation as that they shall do us good instead of harm, and to have the mastery over our appetites, so that we shall command them, and not they us.

I have been speaking of such things as are in themselves harmless, and even useful, but there are other temptations which come under the head of " the flesh," and to which the word "temperate" does not apply, because the soldier of Christ has no right to touch them at all. Such are all those indulgences which tend to blunt the moral sense, and to arouse bad thoughts and passions. These things often come to us under very pretty disguises of art, literature, and the like. I have known a Christian read a vile book, hardly fit for a decent kitchen fire, excusing himself on the ground of the beautiful style— as if one should take poison because it was presented in a finely carved bowl. Christian women go to see other women—young girls, as precious in God's sight as their own daughters— exhibit themselves on the stage in shamelessly indecent dresses and dances. Yes, and they come away and express a virtuous horror of the poor creatures, who are not half as bad as themselves, inasmuch as they are working hard for a living, and not for idle amusement. A shamelessly wicked woman comes among us, and people who profess and call themselves Christians go to see and applaud her on the stage, because, forsooth, it is "an education in art."

In all such matters there is but one rule for the Christian—"touch not, taste not, handle not." Give the enemy no admission under any pretense, however specious. Nobody was ever hurt by letting a doubtful pleasure alone. Our carnal nature will in itself make us trouble enough without any help. By God's grace we can keep it in subjection, but how can we expect that grace, how dare we ask for it, if we run willfully into temptation?

Ps. xvii. 1 Cor. x.

FOURTH THURSDAY IN LENT.

OUR GHOSTLY ENEMY.

IT seems rather the fashion, just now, to deny the existence of Satan as a person at all. I suppose nothing could please him more than to be so denied. "I don't believe in a personal devil," said a lady in a Bible class; "I believe in a principle of evil." When asked to define what she meant by a principle of evil, it appeared that she had no very clear idea of the matter herself. The simple truth is that there is as much proof of the personality of Satan as of the Holy Spirit, and a believer in the Bible may as reasonably deny one as the other. Our Lord always speaks of him as a living, thinking, active being, as in St. John viii. 44, St. Matt. xiii. 19 and 39, and many other places. Try substituting the words " principle of evil " in these passages, and see what sense it will make. Satan is perhaps the most active member of that famous old firm " the world, the flesh, and the devil," in which indeed there are no silent partners. He is always ready to back the others, and, what is still worse, he has a secret ally in every heart, who, though crushed and kept under, is always trying to open correspondence with its old friend. He does not come to us in hideous disguise of hoof and horn, as the old painters have depicted him. None but a fool would do that; and he is no fool as concerns the ends he would compass. " The devil knows many things," says the Arab proverb, " because he is very old." He knows how to put on many disguises, and can on occasions transform himself into an angel of light.

Pride and anger, envy, hatred, and malice, are usually the sins specially attributed to Satan; but there is one class of sins which are particularly his own. I refer to lying in all its branches, to evil-speaking, slander, detraction, and the like. " When he speaketh of a lie, he speaketh of his own, for he is a liar, and the father of it," says our Lord. (St. John viii. 44.) Slander is his business and delight. He is "the accuser of our brethren" (Rev. xii. 10), and the patron of them that do the like.

This matter of evil-speaking is one that deserves grave consideration. It is a common and crying evil. There are probably few —I wish I dared say no—professing Christians who will deliberately invent a slander, but how many are there who will repeat one without a thought, and that of a fellow church-member, with whom they have perhaps knelt at the Lord's table only the day before. Mrs. A. hears a tale of shame concerning a young girl, which, if true, would be enough to blight the young thing's character forever. She does not know if it be true or false; perhaps she does not know the person by sight; but it is a piece of news, and for the dear delight of telling a story she repeats it—never, be it observed, without some slight addition, for few people can repeat a thing exactly as they hear it. Mrs. A. does not think that in so repeating a slander she is making herself responsible for it, but such is the case, and God will hold her so if man does not. She may think herself a very good woman at the very time that she is doing Satan's dirtiest work for him. It is not necessary that slander should always be put into direct words. An insinuation, a lifting of the hands and eyes, nay, silence itself, may and often does say more than words.

"A lie has a thousand legs, while the truth has but two," says the Eastern proverb. No matter how often a false statement is repeated, there is always some one to believe it and repeat it. Here is a notable instance. Some one once said that "every sixpence given to the heathen cost a dollar to send it." It is an utterly false statement, and has been proved so a dozen times; yet it is constantly repeated, and meets the missionary worker at every turn. "I have never cared to have anything to do with Mrs. N., since she was found out taking goods from G.'s store," said a person of one who was a fellow church - member. "But that was entirely disproved," said I, indignantly; "it was shown plainly that Mrs. N. simply took another parcel for her own—a mistake any-one might make." "Oh well, I never heard that!" was the reply. "It was on odd mis-take, anyhow!" I suppose this story will be repeated to Mrs. N.'s discredit for years to come, and not one in twenty who hears it will hear the refutation.

It is a safe rule never to repeat anything to the disadvantage of another, unless abso-lutely necessary. The golden rule applies here as everywhere, "Think, if you are tempted to retail a bit of personal slander, how you would like it if the case were your own—if it were yourself or your wife or daughter that was attacked." Think that every fellow-Christian is a member of the Lord's body, and that in wounding the mem-bers you wound also the Head. Another good rule is never to repeat conversation. We all need the prayer, "Set a watch, O Lord, before my mouth, and keep the door of my lips." (Ps. cxli. 3.) Finally, since it is out of the abundance of the heart that the mouth speaketh, let us strive to keep our hearts and minds as become the temples of the Holy Ghost, pure and clean, and admit no visitors therein but such as are worthy of that greatest and most honored of all guests.

Ps. cxli.   St. James iii.

FOURTH FRIDAY IN LENT.

THE GREAT TEMPTER.

" ONE thing I would not let slip : I took notice that poor Christian was so confounded that he did not know his own voice ; and thus I perceived it.   Just when he was come over against the mouth of the burning pit, one of the wicked ones got behind him, and stepped up sofily to him, and whisperingly suggested many grievous blasphemies to him, which he verily thought had proceeded from his own mind.   This put Christian more to it than anything that he met with before, even to think that he now blasphemed Him that he loved before.   Yet if he could have helped it, he would not have done it; but he had not the discretion either to stop his ears, or to know whence these blasphemies came."

Does not this passage of Bunyan's describe the occasional experience of many a Christian ? We find ourselves assailed by doubts and fears, by hard thoughts of our Father in Heaven, by wicked suggestions of all sorts, till we are ready to despair of ourselves, and to think ourselves hypocrites or castaways.

How it is that Satan contrives to inject these evil suggestions, or why he should be permitted to do so, I cannot tell, any more than I can tell why evil should exist at all. It is a part of that great mystery which may perhaps be explained in a future life, but certainly not here. The practical question is, How are we to meet these assaults, and what is the best way to repel them ?

An old writer has said that the best way to meet temptations is to deal with them as one does with dogs which run out to bark at passengers—walk straight on, and take no notice of them. This is, in many cases, a good rule. Ignore the tempter altogether. Hold no parley with him, but go straight on with whatever you are doing. He will grow tired after a while, and let you alone. But if you must needs fight him—and one cannot always escape the contest—be sure to use the weapons your great Captain has put into your hands, and no other. Take the shield of faith. Repel every doubt with an " I believe" and an "I know." Be sure you are familiar with your sword, which is the Word of God. Above all, never for one moment give up the contest. The Seneca Indians have the correct theory on this subject. They hold that no evil spirit or demon can hurt a man while he fights it, and does not give way to fear; but that if he does so give way, it is all over with him. All the powers of darkness combined cannot drag the weakest disciple from his Saviour's arms so long as the will holds fast to its Lord. Remember this, and show yourselves men.

Remember, too, that there is a sure refuge always at hand, always open, always strong to save. In old times, he who fled for refuge to the altar of the church or temple was safe from his foe. So now, that persecuted saint who takes refuge in the presence of God is in "a little sanctuary." "In the time of trouble He shall hide me in His tabernacle; yea, in the secret place of His dwelling shall He hide me." (Ps. xxvii. 5.) "He shall defend thee under His wings, and thou shalt be safe under His feathers." (Ps. xci. 4) Safe in that sanctuary, and hidden under those wings, we may bid defiance to Satan and all his crew. The Lord shall fight for us, and we shall hold our peace. (Ex. xiv. 14.)

Let us, then, go boldly forward in the race set before us; watchful indeed and wary, but trusting in the power and love of our Captain, who knows our temptations and trials far better than we ourselves. "In that He Himself hath suffered being tempted, He is able to succor them that are tempted." (Heb. ii. 18.) Let us cultivate a sense of God's Presence. Believe me, it is a thing to be cultivated. "If God be for us, who can be against us?" His power is on our side so soon as our will is united to His will by faith and an honest intention.

Let us always remember, for our comfort, that temptations are not sins, else would our Lord not have been without sin. It is only when our wills consent to them that they become so. "You cannot keep those birds from flying over your head," said John Wesley to a young disciple who asked for counsel on this subject, "but you can keep them from making nests in your hair." But never, *never* play or trifle with temptation. Never willfully put yourself in its way. When you do, you give Satan an advantage of which he is not slow to avail himself. It is a story told by some author of antiquity that the devil once entered into a young Christian woman who was present at a show of gladiators. Being summoned to leave her, he refused, declaring that he had found her on his ground, and she was therefore his lawful prey. We may face all the hosts of hell when our Lord's business makes it needful, and we may be sure that in doing so we have the Lord on our side; but if we cross willfully the line between right and wrong in the pursuit of pleasure or business, we have no right to think that God's presence will go with us there. Nay, we should be careful not to approach that line too closely. In time of war, the safe place is not near the front, and above all not on the neutral ground between the armies. There we shall probably be treated as the enemy of both sides. Let our abiding be on the everlasting hills of God's truth and law, where His sun always shines, and where no foe can ever come.

Ps. xci.   1 Peter v.

FOURTH SATURDAY IN LENT.

HEARTINESS.

In the collect which we have been considering, we find an old-fashioned word which means a great deal. We ask God to look upon our *hearty* desires. A hearty desire is one into which we put our whole heart. There may be many things which we would like well enough to have for our own. There are many wishes which we should be pleased to have gratified. But, after all, we do not care enough about them to make any special effort in the matter. But when we heartily desire a thing, we work for it. We take every means to bring about the gratification of our wish, and we do not easily give up and sit down contented without it.

It is so in religious matters. A careless or worldly man may have at times an uneasy feeling that all is not right with him. He hears a rousing sermon perhaps. Some friend or acquaintance dies suddenly, and he won-

ders how he would fare if the same fate
should overtake himself. He thinks he really
will take time to consider the matter at some
future day when he shall not be so busy. He
even tries to pray a little, though he does
not know well how to set about it. But his
heart is not in the matter, and the impres-
sion soon passes away, leaving the man in a
worse case than before; for, be it observed,
nothing hardens the heart like a stifled conviction.

It is to be feared that this half-heartedness
is the true reason why so many prayers are
unanswered, and why so many professed disciples of our Lord have so little comfort in
their religion, and do so little credit to their
profession. They are half-hearted. They
have no earnestness in the matter, and would
even think such earnestness out of place, and
fanatical. They can show and feel enough of
enthusiasm on the subject of a business
enterprise, a game of baseball, a new fashion, a new opera-singer; but speak to such
an one of enthusiasm in religious matters,
and he will look at you in amazement, and
think you a little cracked. He professes to
believe all the articles of the Christian faith,
and bows his head in the creed with all pro-

priety—in church; but talk to him of Heaven
and Hell, of the love of God, and the judg-
ments of God as present realities, and you
make him uncomfortable. He becomes conscious of his own deficiencies, and the feeling
is not agreeable. He will get away as soon
he can, and probably call you a Methodist
behind your back, if he does not do so to
your face.

This half-heartedness is a fatal hindrance
to growth in grace. I fear many pray for
holy hearts, who would, after all, be sorry to
have them. A man prays for grace to cast
away the works of darkness, but there are,
perhaps, certain works of darkness which are
profitable in a business point of view, and he
has no desire to cast them away. A woman
asks that she may perceive and know what
things she ought to do, but she is conscious
of certain duties half hidden in the background of her mind and conscience, on which ·
she does not care to be enlightened, because
the fulfilling of them would be inconvenient.
She prays for grace to withstand the world,
but she does not really wish to withstand it,
because she loves some of its gifts, and does
not mean to throw them away. So people
go on, trying to serve two masters, to please

God and themselves, and getting no real satisfaction from either. They wonder what those mean who talk of the blessedness of service, of communion with God, of comfort in affliction, and the like, and are tempted to regard all such utterances either as fanaticism or pretence, because there is nothing in their own experience to correspond with them.

Is it any wonder that such prayers are not answered, and that such service is not blessed? Would you like it yourself in a child or servant? Surely not.

Let me beg of you, dear fellow-servant of our blessed Master, to examine yourself in this matter, and see if you do not find therein the reason why you have no more comfort in your religion; no more peace and joy and readiness to work for Him who has wrought such great things for us. Is the sign of the cross still on your forehead, or have the kisses of the world worn it away? Do you really and truly *love* God as you love your husband or children, if you have them? Are you ready to sacrifice anything for Him? Suppose that He should offer to release you at this moment from every sin, would you be willing to have Him do it?

This whole-hearted service no doubt has its trials. Our Lord Himself has told us that. "All that would live godly in Jesus Christ shall suffer persecution." (2 Tim. iii. 12.) " If they have called the master of the house Beelzebub, how much more shall they call them of His household ? " (St. Matt. x. 25.) You cannot be faithful to the great King without offending His enemies. You cannot really renounce the world without angering the world. You may not have to meet with such persecutions as the early disciples did, but you will probably be called peculiar, affected, Methodistical. But fear nothing. You may, and probably will, meet with even more serious assaults. Satan will rage when he sees you in earnest, and try his best to bar your path, or win you away from it. But again I say, never fear. The Lord is on your side, and will stretch out His right hand to be your defense. He will feed you with the hidden manna, and give you to drink of the water of Life freely. You shall receive the mystical gift; the white stone wherein is a name written, which no man knoweth saving he that receiveth it. (Rev. ii. 17.) Passing through the valley of misery, you shall use it for a well. The wilderness of this world

8

shall blossom as the rose, and the thorny road lead you surely to the city of the great King.

Isa. xii.   Rev. ii.

FOURTH SUNDAY IN LENT.

REFRESHMENT.

MID-LENT Sunday is also called Refreshment Sunday—a very old name, probably given with reference to the subject of the Gospel for the day, which is the feeding ot the five thousand on the lake of Galilee. Dr. Gouldburn, in his invaluable book on the collects, has shown the connection between the collect, Epistle, and Gospel for the day, all of which are full of matter for reflection. Let us for the present confine our attention to the Gospel, and try, by reverent consideration, to make real to ourselves this wonderful miracle of our Lord's, and see what lesson it has for us.

It had been a time of special activity for our Lord and His more immediate followers. The apostles had just returned from their first preaching mission. Two by two, they

had passed through the lands of Judah and
Galilee, preaching the glad tidings of the
Kingdom of Heaven, healing the sick, restor-
ing the deaf and blind, and casting out evil
spirits in the name of Jesus. I think of two
homely, travel-stained men arriving,at night-
fall, perhaps, in some lonely little village,
and asking the hospitality which was not at
such a time likely to be denied them. There
is nothing about them to distinguish them
from any common wayfarers, as they partake
of the plain fare set before them. But there
is a cloud over the faces of the hosts. The
elder son, the prop of their age, lies on
a bed of sickness, and the physician has said
that there is no release for him save by death.
The guests rise and go to the bedside of the
sufferer, who is perhaps hardly conscious of
their presence, and one of them takes him
by the hand. " In the name of Jesus of Naza-
reth, I bid thee arise and walk." In a moment the dull eyes brighten, the pale cheek
flushes, the helpless limbs feel new life, and
the young man rises, and throws aside the
useless covering, a well man. The amazing
news spreads from house to house, and
soon the whole village is gathered to hear
and see these wonderful strangers. A

woman, weeping over her dead babe, hears the news, and thinks "Oh, had they but come before my child died!" Then a strange ray of hope darts into her mind. The strangers have cured one as good as dead. May they perhaps waken the dead also? At all events, it will do no harm to ask them. She wraps herself in her veil, and goes forth bearing the little waxen corpse, and returns with her child safe and smiling in her arms.

Many such stories must the apostles have had to relate to their Master on their return; some tales, possibly, of rejection and scorn from those they would have blest.

But their meeting was destined to be interrupted by sad tidings. The disciples of John the Baptist had heard of the death of their leader, slain by the wiles of a vile woman. They had been permitted by Herod to pay the last sad duties to his body, and that done there was one thing more remaining to them. They "went and told Jesus." Where could they go, save to that wonderful Being to whom their own revered leader had borne witness, and whose forerunner he had always called himself? We are not told in what words He comforted them. But we know how He showed His consideration for their weariness. "Come ye apart into a desert place, and rest awhile." (S. Mark vi. 31.)

I have often thought, if I were to preach an Ash Wednesday sermon, I would choose these words for my text. It is the call which the Church addresses to her children on that day: "Come!" she says; "Come from the hurry of business, and the worse and more distracting hurry of pleasure. Leave your cares behind you for a time. Let the world take care of itself. It will do well enough without you, as it did before you were born, and will do after you are dead. Come into a desert place as yet unspoiled by man, and rest awhile."

We are apt to think of a desert as a barren and sandy waste, destitute of verdure or beauty; but this is not its usual meaning in the Bible. It simply denotes an uncultivated tract, often used as pasture, and covered with grass and flowers in the season. It was to such a place as this that Jesus now retired with the disciples; to the narrow green plain of El Batihah, as it is now called. It was a spot about six miles from Capernaum by sea, surrounded by high hills, and quite uninhabited. Here the weary band might hope for a season of quiet and refreshment.

But they were destined to be disappointed. The boat, retarded probably by contrary winds, seems to have made but slow progress, and when they did at last arrive, they found the ground occupied by an eager crowd, waiting for the healer, of whose powers they had already made proof.

Here was a disappointment indeed! But our Lord shewed no irritation at the failure of His plan. He " was moved with compassion toward them, because they were as sheep not having a shepherd; and He began to teach them many things " (St. Mark vi. 34), and He also healed their sick.

Here is at once a practical lesson to be learned from our Lord's conduct—I mean that of patience under interruption and disappointment. We make a plan, for some good enterprise probably, and straightway that plan becomes, as it were, something sacred in our eyes, and we are not only grieved, but vexed, if anything happens to hinder us. We feel in our secret souls, if we do not venture to say so, that we are hardly treated, and we are ready to say, nay, perhaps we do say, that we will never undertake any such thing again.

In truth, there are interruptions which it

is hard to bear with patience; for instance, the way in which idle people take up the time of busy people with the veriest trifles.

Yet all these things are part of our life's trials, and must be met in the right spirit, and turned to some account. In respect to our plans, the right way, it seems to me, is to sit loosely to them, with a reference in all things to a Will higher than ours. "If the Lord will, we shall do this or that." (St. James iv. 15.) If He takes us away from one piece of work, it may be because He has something better or more important for us to do; or that His wisdom sees that this particular work is better left undone. If your plan has been made with due regard to His glory, depend upon it He will not suffer it to fail utterly.

With regard to those interruptions from idle people of which I have spoken, we may be able to turn even them to account. We may try to give the conversation a serious and profitable turn. We may have a chance of defending the absent or the calumniated, or of recommending some good work. At worst we can let patience have her perfect work, and thus grow more like that Master

whom it is at once our most important work
and our dearest wish to imitate.

Ex. xvii.   St. John vi. 1–21.

FOURTH MONDAY IN LENT.

REFRESHMENT SUNDAY—*Continued.*

ALL day long our Lord was engaged in
teaching the people, and in healing their
sick. The fact that he did so teach this great
multitude of common people, and that they
heard Him gladly, as we know they did (St.
Mark xii. 37), is surely a sufficient answer to
those who talk about the danger of giving
the Scriptures to the unlearned. Meantime
the disciples no doubt were reposing as they
shared in their Lord's instructions, and wit-
nessed His miracles. But as the afternoon
of that long spring day drew on to its close
they began to be uneasy. They looked
abroad over the vast multitude thronging
the plain, and wondered how they were to
be fed and lodged, "for divers of them came
from afar," and there were women and children among them, some of whom, no doubt,
had just been cured of severe illness. We

can see them consulting together with anxious faces, and many a troubled glance at the Master, and at last they venture to remind Him of the lateness of the hour, and the loneliness of the place where they were. "This is a desert place and the time is far spent ; send them away, that they may buy food." (St. Mark vi. 36.) But the Lord had his own purposes to fulfill, and he answered them tranquilly, "They need not depart ; give ye them to eat;" and then, as if their astonishment were not enough at such a proposition under such circumstances, He turns to Philip with the question, "Whence shall we buy bread, that these may eat ?"

Philip must have been indeed amazed at the question. Buy bread for that great crowd of people ! True, there was a market not so very far away, in the little city of Bethsaida Julius, but it might be doubtful whether so small a place could furnish the requisite quantity of bread, even if they had the means to pay for it. "Two hundred pennyworth is not sufficient for them, that every one of them might take a little ; " and one of the number asks, "Shall we go and buy bread ?"

Andrew, whose natural disposition seems to have been of that helpful sort which always moves the owner thereof to do something practical, here makes a suggestion. While others had been talking he had been investigating the resources at hand, and he now comes forward leading a little boy, and announces the result of his inquiries. " There is a lad here who has five barley loaves and two small fishes." (St. John vi. 9.) With what amazed looks his fellow-disciples must have regarded him ! Only five loaves and two fishes ! He himself was conscious of the seeming absurdity, for he added immediately, " What are they among so many ?" What, indeed ! Hardly enough for two, and here were thousands.

But as the disciples regarded our Lord's face they must have been in some measure reassured. There was no embarrassment or uncertainty to be read there. He Himself knew what He would do, as His next words showed them : " Make the men sit down." Here, at least, was a plain, practical command, and cheerfully they hastened to obey.

In all our perplexities and puzzles we can usually find something to do at once, and that something leads to something else, till by degrees the way is made plain before us. The old Saxon motto, "Do the next thing," is the guide out of many a difficulty. "How are we ever to fill this box?" said one of the officers of a certain missionary auxiliary; "we have only money enough to buy half a dozen towels." "Very well, let us buy the towels," was the answer; "by the time they are hemmed we shall have more." And so it proved; and a better box never gladdened a hard-working woman than was sent to that faithful teacher. A poor woman in England once gave a few shillings, the result of long saving, to purchase some Bibles for the poor; and out of that gift grew one of the great Bible societies which supply the Scriptures to hundreds of thousands. A few serious words, kindly spoken to a wild young man in a diligence, gave to the Moravian Church one of the most successful missionaries that ever lived. Let us use what we have. It may be not so much as the little lad brought in his basket, but the Master will accept it and use it; whether it be to the feeding of one or ten thousand does not signify, so it is to His service. Let us take the first step in obedience to His command, and the next step will be made plain. It may be but a short one, but it will be so much in advance. Like the pilgrim in the valley of the shadow

of death, when we lift up our foot to go forward, we may not know where, or upon what
we may set it next ; but be sure the solid
ground will be there to meet it, so long as
we are in the way of the Celestial City.

1 Kings xvii.   Acts xvii. 16.

FOURTH TUESDAY IN LENT.

REFRESHMENT SUNDAY—*Continued.*

"Now there was much grass in the place."
So the men sat down in orderly ranks or
companies—an arrangement made by our
Lord's own command, that they might be
the more easily waited upon. The word
used by St. Mark signifies parterres, or the
orderly arrangement of the plants in a vine-
yard or garden, and the assembly, dressed
in the gay colors which Orientals affect, must
have looked somewhat like a great flower-
garden. Doubtless, all faces were eagerly
turned toward our Lord, as the people wondered what was coming next. The disciples
gathered round their Master, amazed, no
doubt, but ready to obey His order, whatever it might be ; and near Him, perhaps,

stood the little lad who had brought the provision, his eyes fixed on that face which ever had an attraction for children. Jesus took in His hands the cakes of barley bread, "and when He had given thanks, He brake them, and began to distribute them to the disciples, and they to the people, and likewise of the fishes, as much as they would." (St. John vi. 11.) The original words seem to show that the provisions were multiplied in our Lord's hands. Here was a sudden end of all their perplexities. Here was enough and to spare, of palatable and wholesome food. It must have been with glad hearts that the twelve, aided, no doubt, by the disciples of John, passed around among the people bearing the unexpected refreshment. Doubtless the multitude shared in their joy. for many of them were far from their homes; and the prospect of returning hungry, or possibly of spending the night supperless in the open air, could not have been very agreeable. It is no great wonder, perhaps, that as they partook of His bounty, the old idea of making the Lord a temporal ruler should have recurred to their minds. Surely one who could so wonderfully provide for his followers would have no difficulty in defying

the power even of the Romans.   It was long
before the Lord's immediate and trusted disciples realized the fact that His kingdom
was not of this world.

But the people had eaten all they needed.
What next?   The next command must also
have somewhat surprised both the disciples
and the people.   " Gather up the fragments,
that nothing be lost." Why this exact econ-
omy on the part of one who could, as they
had just seen, produce food at will?   However, the disciples obeyed without a question, and soon they had filled twelve of the
satchels, which all strict Jews carried when
on a journey (to protect their food from
ceremonial uncleanness), with the fragments
which remained of the loaves and fishes.
And now their work was for the present finished.   Jesus would be alone for a time ; and
he dismissed His immediate followers to go
to the other side of the lake, while He Himself sent the multitude away.   The disciples
seemed to have been somewhat unwilling to
leave their Lord alone, but His will was law,
and they betook themselves to the boat
which had brought them hither.   When the
multitude had at last departed, doubtless
with many a lingering look behind, He who

had so cheerfully given up His own plan of
rest and retirement for the sake of teaching
and feeding them, departed into a mountain
to pray. At last He was alone ; and how
grateful to His weary senses must have been
the solemn quiet and dewy freshness of that
mountain solitude ! How dear to His heart
the opportunity of holding undisturbed communion with His Father! Dear tired mother
or teacher, or busy housekeeper, are your
senses also weary and your nerves unstrung
with perpetual din ? Do you, too, long for
solitude and silence? Remember that the
Lord has been before you in this trial also.
The most of His active life was passed in a
crowd, almost always careless and unsympa-
thizing, often captious and hostile ; and His
hours of devotion must be stolen from needed
sleep.

"Each pang from irritation, turmoil, din,"
is known to Him, and He will give needed
help and relief.

Our Lord gave thanks before He distributed the bread to the disciples. This was an
universal custom among the Jews, and the
Lord has approved it by His example. "He
who enjoys anything without a blessing, robs
God," says the Talmud. Yet how many

Christian families are there in which grace before meat is never heard. It looks a little, indeed, as if family religion, of any sort, were to become a thing of the past. The father hastens to his business, and the children to their school, without one word of recognition for the mercies of the night; without a single petition for help and guidance through the day. The father is, or should be, the priest of his own household, to offer up their spiritual sacrifices; but how many never think of doing so! He should be their instructor in divine things; but how many never open the Bible with their children! The boys see their father busy till the last stroke of the church bell with his Sunday papers; they see the same papers or a novel taken up on his return. Is it any wonder that they come to think religion a matter of secondary importance? Is it any wonder that they think it fit only for women, since they see its outward observance left wholly to them? Oh, how many thorns are these negligent, indifferent Christian fathers and mothers cultivating for their own pillows! It is true that a boy or girl may turn out badly, however much pains has been taken with the religious training, because in this world all must make the choice between good and evil for themselves; but at least the careful, conscientious parent has not the added bitter pang of thinking "my neglect, my selfish indulgence, has made the child what he is."

"Gather up the fragments," said our Lord. He could create at will enough to feed five thousand, yet He would not have the remainder lost. With what displeasure must He not look on the lavish wastefulness of His children. Some man takes a good religious paper, or more than one. Perhaps he finds time to glance at them, perhaps not. The expenditure of a cent a week, or the sending of a child or servant, would carry that paper to some poor man or woman— perhaps to some one shut up with illness— who would be only too glad to read it. But no one thinks of that, and what might give aid and comfort to God's afflicted or hard-worked child goes to the ragman. The partly worn hose or flannel garment share the same fate, when a little of the time given to some useless bit of fancy work would make them fit to bestow on some poor body, or to help out a hospital box. I knew a lady with a family of sons. When their socks or underwear were thrown aside, she had them carefully mended and put away in a special place; and many a poor hard-working woman was helped out of Mrs. Z.'s "give-away drawer." We have no right to waste, because all that we have, whether of time or goods or talent, is not ours, but our Lord's. We are but His stewards, and it is required of stewards that a man be found faithful.

Prov. xxxi.   St. Luke xiv.

FIFTH WEDNESDAY IN LENT.

COMFORT.

A CERTAIN writer has said that there is no more beautiful word in the language than the word "comfort." Certainly there is none which carries with it more meanings, or one which it is harder to define. Rest from weariness, freedom from pain, security from danger, all these are comprised in the word "comfort." But these are, after all, but negative, and there is a positive side. The word often means consolation. "As one whom his mother comforteth, so will I comfort you," is God's promise to His people. (Isa. lxvi. 13.) Think of a little child waking in the dark, from some dream of terror. The darkness is all around him, with its possibilities of danger. Who knows what it may hide in those dark corners, behind those dimly seen, waving curtains ? He can feel no one near him. To his excited fancy it seems as if he were alone in the universe, and he cries out in fear and anguish. But in a moment a tender arm is laid over him, a warm kiss reassures him, a well-known voice speaks his name, and he sinks to sleep again, sure that no evil thing can harm him, because his mother is there to be his defense.

So it often is with the Christian. He walks in the midst of trouble. Darkness is around and within. His purposes are broken off, his plans even for his Master's service are frustrated, and, what seems to make his trouble worst of all, he is hampered by indifference, if not by open hostility on the part of fellow-Christians and fellow-church-members. He says to himself, with David, " It is not an enemy that hath done me this dishonor ; but it was even thou, my companion, my guide, and mine own familiar friend." He feels almost as if His Lord Himself had forgotten him, and he is ready to sit down in despair.

But by and by a ray of light falls athwart the darkness. It is the hour for his regular devotion, and he will not neglect it. His heart feels cold and dead, if not absolutely rebellious, but at least he can obey, and he takes up his Bible or his prayer-book, opens perhaps to the thirty-seventh Psalm, or some other like it.

He reads precious promises of help and protection, and deliverance from trouble, such as these. "Commit thy way unto the Lord, and put thy trust in Him, and He shall bring it to pass. He shall make thy righteousness as clear as the light and thy just dealing as the noon-day." (Ps. xxxvii. 5.) He is made to see that he is but tasting the edge, as it were, of that cup which his Master drained to the dregs for him. He feels that God has not forsaken him, and he is by and by able to say, "In the multitude of the sorrows that I had in my heart, Thy comforts have refreshed my soul." The assurance comes to him that the Lord will use all to His own glory and the good of His servant, and he is content to tarry the Lord's leisure.

Or take another case. The Christian is made aware that he has fallen into sin. He has spoken unadvisedly with his lips perhaps, and fears that his words may do great harm. He has given way to unjust or excessive anger, or he has been led into some worldly compliance which he now sees to have been wrong. Or, worse still, he has suddenly awakened to the fact that he has for a long time been declining in godliness, that he has been living for the world and not for his Master. He has gone out of the way into By-path meadow, and the road, which at first seemed to run close to the highway, has turned aside till he has come at least within sight of the dwelling of Giant Despair. Satan is not slow to take advantage of his fall. He tells the sinner that it is plain to be seen that he never was a true disciple. Could one who had really tasted of the grace of God so dishonor his profession? Or if he were once a child of God, is it not as plain as day that he is so no longer? Has he not come too far out of the way ever to find his path back? Will he be received even if he should return? Is this the return he has made to God for all his benefits, and can such black ingratitude ever be forgiven? Such suggestions as these drive the sinner almost to desperation. Almost, but not

quite. His very agony and distress teach
him how precious was that Lord from whom
he has turned away, and he will not give him
up without a struggle at least.

But he is not left to struggle alone. God
has not forgotten His child, though that
child may for a time have forgotten Him.
He may leave him, or seem to leave him, to
suffer for a time the penalty of his sins ; for
as many as the Lord loves, He rebukes and
chastises. But let the sinner once accept
the punishment of his iniquity (Lev. xxvi.
41) ; let him acknowledge that he is justly
punished for his offenses, as says the collect
for the day, and light begins to dawn on the
night of despair. He, too, opens his Bible,
and he reads such words as these, " Though
your sins be as scarlet, they shall be as
white as snow." (Isa. i. 18.) " If we confess
our sins, He is faithful and just to forgive
us our sins, and to cleanse us from all unrighteousness." (1 John i. 9.) " Him that
cometh unto Me, I will in no wise cast out."
(St. John vi. 37.) And so he casts himself at
the feet of his crucified Lord, humbly bewailing his sinfulness, and asking pardon for the
sake of that very love that he has outraged
and grieved. Humbly he believes his prayer

is accepted, trusting in God's unchanging promise, though he has for the present no evidence in his own feelings that his sins are pardoned. By and by the light grows clearer. He hears within a sweet voice, sweeter than any music of earth, whisper such precious words as these: "I, even I, am He that blotteth out thy transgressions for mine own sake, and will not remember thy sins." (Isa. xliii. 25.) Then the Sun of righteousness riseth on His soul with healing in His wings, and it is day.

Ps. xxxii.   St. John xvii.

FIFTH THURSDAY IN LENT.

THE SOURCES OF COMFORT.

THE first source of comfort to the disciple in distress is his general confidence in the goodness of his Lord. "Comfort them with a sense of Thy goodness!" asks the collect for the sick and the afflicted in the prayer-book ; and there is not in that whole wonderful volume a sentence more full of meaning. "My Father is all-wise, therefore He cannot make a mistake; He is perfectly holy, therefore He cannot do an unjust thing; He is perfect love, therefore He will never do a cruel thing; and He sees and cares for me as much as if I were the only child for whom He had to care." Thoughts like these come to the pilgrim, bowed down by the burden and heat of the day ; and they give him courage to take up his load and struggle on toward that rest which remains for the people of God—that mansion prepared for him, and whose roofs and towers his faith sees above the clouds, gleaming in Heaven's own sunshine. To souls like this it does indeed come to pass that, going through the valley of misery, they use it for a well, and the pools are filled with water. "Their light affliction, which is for a moment, worketh for them a far more exceeding weight of glory," because "they look not at the things which are seen, but at those things which are unseen and eternal." (2 Cor. iv. 17.)

The second source of comfort to the Christian which we shall consider is the written word of God. "In the Lord's word will I comfort me." (Ps. lvi. 10.) Here is the sure holding-ground for the anchor of faith. Our feelings are the sport of every wind that blows, but the written word remains, and remains ever the same. The stricken woman whose prop and stay has been taken away, perhaps in a moment, and who knows not where to turn for help, may read in that Word that God is the God of the fatherless, and defendeth the cause of the widow. (Ps. lxviii. 5.) The invalid, wearied out with the life-long pain, which has become such an old story that people no longer think of asking about it, who feels faith ready to fail, and courage to give way under the load, to such an one comes the message, "My grace is sufficient for thee, for my strength is made perfect in weakness." (2 Cor. xii. 9.) The aged saint bowed beneath the burden of years, perhaps with no child or near friend to support his weakness and bear with his infirmities, prays, "Forsake me not when I am gray-headed" (Ps. lxxi. 18), and the Word which supplies the prayer answers it with a corresponding promise, "Even to your old age I am He ; and even to hoary hairs will I carry you." (Is. xlvi. 4.) The repentant, all but despairing sinner, is told by that very righteous and holy God whom he hath so grievously offended, "I, even I, am He that blotteth out thy transgressions for mine

own sake, and will not remember thy sins."
(Is. xliv. 22.) And again, "The blood of
Jesus Christ cleanseth us from all sin." (1
John i. 7.) The backslider reads, "I will
heal their backslidings ; I will love them
freely." (Hosea xiv. 4.) And to the child of
God, striving in meekness and faithfulness
to follow in the steps of his Lord and Master, and to do his commonplace, every task
for Him, the words of cheer and strength are
not to be counted.

The worship and ordinances of the Church
are perennial springs of help and cheer to
the Christian. I appeal to your experience,
faithful fellow-disciples. How many times,
when it has perhaps been a great effort to go
to church, has not the very stillness of the
place fallen like balm on your tired nerves,
so that your few minutes of mental prayer
have made you able to realize that you are
indeed in the presence of Him who has said,
" When two or three are gathered together,
there am I in the midst of them"! (Matt.
xviii. 20.) How often has the Psalter or the
lesson contained the very words you needed!
How often has the sermon or address been
just what you wanted, and the whole service
sent you home strengthened and cheerful to

take up the burden of the week or the day!
Then there is the crown of all our services—
the Holy Communion. We " do not feel like
going," perhaps. We have had but little
time for preparation. There has been much
in the week to harass and perplex us. Perhaps some slip or fall has clouded our experience, and burdened our conscience. But
we know our duty, and at least we can obey.
We carry our burden, whatever it may be,
into the presence of the symbols of our
Lord's dying love ; perhaps to the very
altar rail; but when we rise from our knees,
we find we have left it there.

Isa. lxv. 2 Cor. i.

FIFTH FRIDAY IN LENT.

THE GREAT CONSOLER.

"THE Comforter which is the Holy Ghost."
The third Person of the ever-blessed Trinity
does not disdain to take the title and office
of our consoler, as well as that of our teacher
and guide. He does not disdain to enter the
lowest dwelling which is open to receive
Him, nor to hold communion with the

youngest and feeblest who seek His aid. It is He who opens our heart to understand the Scriptures, who directs us to the very word we need, who shows us, in some passage we have read a hundred times, a new meaning which we never saw before. It is He who inspires our prayers, and He, when our hearts are too burdened for words, makes intercession for us with groanings which cannot be uttered. (Rom. viii. 26.) How are we to obtain the help of this Divine Comforter? First, by asking for it. That is one of the prayers certain to be answered, whatever is refused. " If ye, then, being evil, know how to give good gifts to your children, how much more shall your Heavenly Father give the Holy Spirit to them that ask Him "! (St. Luke xi. 13.) The very greatest gift of all is never refused to the poorest suppliant. Then, when we have invited our guest, we must make our house ready to receive Him. We must open the door and be on the watch for Him. We must remember, too, that He will never share a divided throne. If we are entertaining any impure or unworthy guests —if we have set up any idols there—if there is within any chamber of imagery where we pay secret worship, as did the elders of Israel whom Ezekiel saw in his vision (Ezek. viii. 7–10), the guests must be turned out, the idols overthrown, the secret chamber opened to the light of God's day, before the Spirit of purity will make our heart His shrine. He Himself will purify His own temple if we consent thereto, but we must be willing, and we must have no reserves from Him.

Again, we must be willing to obey His godly motions, as the collect has it, and that with a prompt and willing obedience. This is not always easy or agreeable. One of His offices is to convince of sin, of righteousness, and of judgment to come. He does not always prophecy smooth things, by any means, nor does he always apply sweet balms. On the contrary, He is a kind but stern surgeon, who wounds to heal, and gives bitter tonics instead of soothing syrups. It is not altogether pleasant to be told that some favorite habit is a sinful indulgence; that some yielding to the customs of society is conformity to the world; some laxity of doctrine, on which we have perhaps prided ourselves as showing our liberality, is a cowardly surrender of God's truth. Nevertheless must the Heavenly monitor be obeyed, and that promptly. Otherwise His voice will grow fainter and fainter and fainter, till it ceases to be heard at all. Nay, it is possible to drive away the Heavenly visitor altogether, and then woe unto us. We had better lose every earthly friend than to be forsaken of the Holy Spirit.

It is to be feared that many Christians do not realize as they ought the blessed fact of the real literal indwelling of the Holy Ghost. They read in the Bible such words as these : "He dwelleth with you, and shall be in you." (St. John xiv. 17.) "We have received not the spirit of the world, but the Spirit which is of God." (1 Cor. ii. 12.) They feel as if it were a kind of presumption to take these promises to themselves—as if the real presumption did not lie in doubting, instead of believing God's word. They read such words as these : "The spirit itself beareth witness with our spirits that we are the children of God." (Rom. viii. 16.) Yet they feel no assurance of their adoption, but go through life, as it were, with a rope round their necks instead of walking freely as God's children should, for "where the Spirit of the Lord is, there is liberty." (2 Cor. iii. 17.)

But some one says : "I should be only too glad to obtain this blessed assurance of salvation, but I do not know how. What is the way?" The way is as plain as are all God's ways in things of practical importance to us. You have but to put out your hand and take what is freely offered you.

A vessel sailing to Brazil once saw a barque flying a signal of distress, and bearing down on her, asked what was the matter. "For God's sake, give us water! we have not had a drop for three days," was the cry from the distressed vessel. The answer was instant. "Let down your bucket and draw it up, man! You are in the mouth of the Amazon." These poor creatures had been dying of thirst for three days, though they were sailing on the greatest stream of fresh water in the world, because they had lost their reckoning and did not know where they were. So it too often is with the disciple. He walks in the midst of unnumbered blessings. The stream of living water flows at his side ; the tree of Life grows beside it ; yet he is hungry and thirsty, just because he will not take the things which are freely offered of God. "If ye will not believe, surely ye shall not be established." (Isa. vii. 9.)

Ps. lxiii.   Gal. v.

FIFTH SATURDAY IN LENT.

THE USE OF COMFORT.

"SURELY there can be no question about that !" I hear some one say.

"The use of comfort is to make people comfortable." That is one use, no doubt, but not the only nor the principal one. It is to be feared, however, that many sincerely devout people take this view of the matter. In spiritual as in worldly matters we are prone to think far too much of our own enjoyment. Some good people, indeed, measure their spiritual condition by their enjoyment. If they are happy, they think all is well with them. This is not always a safe test. We may be glorying in a very mistaken estimate of our own spiritual condition, as did the Corinthian Church, when St. Paul wrote them. "Your glorying is not good." They were mightily puffed up in their own esteem, while they were tolerating among them the vilest sins, such as even the idolatrous Gentiles were ashamed of. (1 Cor. v. 1–8.)

The use of comfort is to strengthen us for the work which God gives us to do. " The God of all comfort comforteth us in all our tribulation," writes St. Paul; and why ? " That we may be able to comfort them which are in any trouble, by the comfort wherewith we ourselves are comforted of God." (2 Cor. i. 3, 4.) We are comforted that we may be able to console others, just as we are taught in order that we may teach others.

Dear fellow-sufferer, if in your sick-room your Lord has sent you a blessing, cannot you contrive to send that blessing on to some other sufferer ? He has sent you, let us say, a cheering message by a book or paper. Can you not pass it on to some one else ? He has given you a cheering thought. Can you not give a friend or attendant the benefit of it ? Some one brings you a pattern for embroidery or knitting. It will do you all the more good if you use it to make a Christmas gift for some other invalid who does not enjoy as many pretty things as yourself. A lady of my acquaintance once received from a wealthy and generous friend a box of very fine forced strawberries. She sent a part of them to an old lady in a charitable institution, whose failing appetite could hardly be tempted to take food at all. The sight of a dish of strawberries in March was such a wonder that it led her to eat quite a good meal; and a year afterwards she spoke with delight of "those beautiful berries your mother sent me." I mention this as a specimen of the way a kindness may be passed on. I believe that act of thoughtful kindness prolonged for several years a useful life.

There are those who carry an atmosphere of comfort with them wherever they go. They may not be very brilliant or very accomplished, but every one is glad to see them. They have something pleasant to say. Such a person does not tell a rheumatic patient of her grandmother who was unable to feed herself for years, or suggest to one suffering from a surgical operation that people in such circumstances almost always go into a decline. (I have known of these very things being done more than once.) I once suffered for several months from the effects of a cat's bite, and I suppose that more than half the people to whom the story was told said, "I should think you would be afraid of hydrophobia!" With a nervous or apprehensive person the effect might have been serious. Oh how many heartaches and tears would be saved to invalids, if those who visit them would try to think of something pleasant and cheering to say!

God sends us comfort, not that we may sit down and selfishly enjoy it, but that we may be strengthened for the work which is still before us, whether that work be active doing, or patient suffering, or quietly waiting on His will. Comfort is not an end, but a means, and it is much more likely to last if we use it in this way, than if we sit idly down to enjoy it. The Lord gives to all his children blessed seasons of rest and enjoyment. As the twenty-third Psalm says, He makes them to lie down in green pastures, and feedeth them by still waters. But He does not always keep us there. He sets before them many a hill to climb, many a dark valley to pass through, before we reach the land of Beulah, and the Celestial city. But the Holy Ghost, which is the comforter, will always abide with us, and we can truly say "In the multitude of sorrows which I had in my heart, Thy comforts have refreshed my soul." (Ps. xciv. 19.)

Ps. xxxvii.   Heb. xii.

FIFTH SUNDAY IN LENT.

THE GOVERNMENT OF GOD.

It has been said, and I think truly, that almost any government is better than none. A good government is an unspeakable blessing—not always appreciated, I fear, by those who have never lived under any other. Think for a moment what it is to dwell under a rule where every one's rights are safe; where no one can be punished, except openly, and by due process of law ; where every poor man's house is his castle ; where, amid the excitement of a hotly contested election, women and children walk the streets in absolute safety: and then contrast this state of things with one in which no man, great or small, feels himself secure; where any man or woman may be torn from home and friends and thrown into prison or sent into life-long exile, with no chance of redress, and knowing that the nearest and dearest friends are utterly ignorant of the fate of husband or wife, father or mother. It seems to me a pity that those who complain so bitterly of the few abuses of a good and free government, should not for a little while try the tender mercies of a bad one.

The best government, however, being as it is the work of man, is liable to imperfection in its constitution, or abuse in its administration. How happy, then, is he who lives under a ruler who can and will do no wrong. Such a ruler is the Lord our Governor. The best of earthly governments can only legislate for classes, and even beneficent laws often bear hardly on individuals ; but God's rule is that of a father, who sees in each person not only a subject, but a child ; who knows the needs of each one better than himself, and who grudges His children no innocent pleasure. Is it any wonder that the Church teaches us to pray for the rule of such a sovereign as a blessing ?

In translating this collect from the Latin original, the reformers have substituted the words " Thy people " for " Thy family," thinking, probably, that the word corresponded better with the idea of government. But, after all, a family needs a stable and just government as much as a state, and it is as a family that the Lord rules his people. The

state lays down an inflexible rule, to which
every citizen is expected to conform ; but a
wise parent does not act in this way. She
studies the disposition of each child, and has
a different system for each one, corresponding to its temperament and needs. So it is
with God's government. To Him there are
no " masses." He does not drive His flock
like a mercenary drover, but " He calleth His
own sheep by name and leadeth them out."
(St. John x. 3.) He is to each one what He
is to no other. " To him that overcometh
will I give to eat of the hidden manna, and
will give him a white stone, and in the stone
a new name written, which no man knoweth
saving he that receiveth it." (Rev. ii. 17.)

The state punishes offenses against the
laws with rigid severity, and very rightly.
The security of the honest citizen demands
such action. But it has no thanks and no
praise for the obedient and loyal subject. He
has but done what was expected of him. The
loyal subject of God's government, on the
contrary, has the satisfaction of knowing
that his ruler sees his obedience, and is gratified with it. Like Enoch, he has this tes-
timony, that he has pleased God. God notes
the first effort of a little child as well as the

crowning sacrifice of an Abraham, and rewards the poor negro Sunday-school teacher, trying in imperfect English to tell the little he knows about God and the Bible to some one more ignorant than himself, as He does a St. Paul preaching to the polished Athenians on Mars Hill. Surely there must be, to the believer, wonderful joy and strength in the thought that what he does gives pleas- to his Heavenly Father.

There is no escaping from the government of God. A man who is dissatisfied with the rule of the United States, or who by crime or misdemeanor has brought himself within reach of its penalties, may go and live somewhere else ; but there is no getting out of this universe, which God rules in every corner. Neither can he escape by denying God's authority, or making light of His claims. The earthly commonwealth admits no such excuse ; much less the Heavenly. The man may rebel furiously. He may wish that it were possible even to pull down the great Ruler from His throne. It makes no difference. He has no choice but to submit at last, but he *has* the choice as to whether his submission shall be that of the criminal on his way to the scaffold, or the glad obe-

dience of the loving child who has full confidence in his father's justice and love.

Ps. xcvii.   Phil. i.

FIFTH MONDAY IN LENT.

CÆSAR'S HOUSEHOLD.

THE Lord's government, as we have seen,
is that of a parent, in that He legislates, not
for masses, but for individuals ; and His object, in all that He does and leaves undone,
is to make His children better and in the
long run happier. The views and plans of
the wisest parent are necessarily bounded
by a very limited horizon, but the Lord sees
the lives of His children from their first
beginning—not indeed to the end, for there
is no end, but to the farthest reach of eternity—and He legislates for them in "the
whole of their duration," as President Ed-
wards has it. It is perhaps for this reason,
speaking with reverence, that Christians
often find themselves in about the last places
they themselves would have chosen as likely
to conduce to growth in grace. We are apt
to fret at this, and to think we could do

much better somewhere else. We think if
we could only attend such and such a church,
or live in some other place, or attend such
and such classes, we could do so much better ; and, very possibly, we neglect the work
that God has given us for something which
is not our work at all.

There is a passage in the Epistle to the
Philippians which at first sight may appear
to mean very little, but which seems to me
very suggestive. St. Paul, writing from his
prison at Rome to the church at Philippi,
says, " All the saints salute you, chiefly they
that are of Cæsar's household." (Phil. iv. 22.)

Surely this was a very strange place in
which to look for saints—about the last
place, humanly speaking, in which we should
be likely to find them. The Cæsar was
Nero—a name which has become a synonym
for lust, cruelty, and rampant folly of every
kind ; and his court was just what we should
expect the court of such an emperor to be.
It was the very central resort of murderers,
informers, men and women practiced in every
namable and un - namable wickedness of
that vile age. One would as soon have
looked for the bliss of Paradise in the foulest
pool of Dante's hell, as for saints in such a

household, especially when the profession of the Christian faith involved no little danger to liberty and life. The persecution of Christians had not at that time reached the height to which it attained afterwards; nevertheless, every Christian was looked upon with suspicion and contempt. Their great teacher and apostle was a prisoner, chained night and day to a soldier who watched him, and his imprisonment was more than likely to end in an ignominious death. Yet, in spite of these opposing circumstances, there were saints in Cæsar's household, and, it would seem, not a few.

It seems to me that we may all learn a good lesson from this short passage. We are so apt to lay our shortcomings to the account of circumstances, which is, in fact, laying them at the door of Providence. " If I were not so much engrossed in business," says John. "If I had not so many family cares," says Jane, " I might do some Church work." " There is no pleasure in going to church and Bible class here," says another. " If I only lived in the city! we cannot expect to do much in a place like this," I heard a Christian man say. " If we had a first-class preacher and a good quartette choir we might do something." As if the gift of the Holy Spirit depended on a fine preacher and a fine choir ! But we do more than this: we lay upon circumstances the blame of our own heart sins. We should not be irritable and fretful, only that there is so much to annoy us. We should not make unkind remarks and tell scandalous stories about our neighbors, only that every one does so ; and so on to the end of the chapter. No Christian will deny, if asked the question out and out, that his Father in Heaven has ordered, or at the least permitted, the circumstances of his life. Say that we are placed in a country parish, where there is little or no enthusiasm for any good cause, and where most of the parishioners think they have done their duty nobly when they have helped to keep their pastor on the outside verge of starvation, instead of the inside. Well, He places us there because He has work for us there—some work which no one could do so well as you or I. Let us try to find out what that work is, and to do it faithfully. We shall grow in grace ourselves, and no one can do that without benefiting others. Or He has put one of His chosen ones in a place where he has no Christian

sympathy—perhaps among unbelievers and
scoffers. Take courage. Bad as they may
be, they are probably saints themselves,
compared to the men and women with whom
they of Cæsar's household were brought in
daily contact. You may have good work
to do among them. A little leaven leaveneth
the whole lump. When the Rev. Mr. Low-
der entered the district of St. Peter's, in
the east of London, there were not a dozen
Christian men in the parish. He was hooted
and pelted in the street, and on one occasion a ring of his friends had to fight for his
life against a howling mob of ruffians. Every
other house was a house of ill-fame; when
he died, after twenty-three years' service,
there was not one such to be found in the
parish; and by the streets where he had been
stoned and all but murdered, he was carried
to his burial through throngs of weeping
men and women, hundreds of whom walked
miles to see him laid in the grave.

A little leaven leaveneth the whole lump.
But, then, the leaven must be living and
warm. Frozen yeast is no good, as every
housewife knows. "I got my father and
mother to come to church last Sunday,"
said a dear little child with sparkling eyes.

"It was so nice!" He had been laboring for that result for months. He would have been one of the saints in Cæsar's household. And I have no doubt that those saints found there, were of a pretty robust and earnest description. *They* would hardly have stayed away from the gathering in St. Paul's cabin on the first day of the week because they had not the latest fashion in gown or sandal, or even to hear the court poet recite his ode, or to learn the last news from Gaul or Britain. (2 Kings v.; 1 Peter ii.)

A part of this chapter was printed in the Kalendar.

FIFTH TUESDAY IN LENT.

THE HOUSEHOLD OF GOD.

As has been noticed before, the reformers, in translating this collect from the original Latin, saw fit to render the word "familiam," that is to say, household or family, by "people," thinking probably that the word corresponded better to the idea of government. It is perhaps difficult to see the aptness of the change, since, as has been observed, a family certainly needs governing quite as much as a state.

In three other places is the Church of God spoken of as a family. In the collect for Good Friday we beseech God to behold "this His family." In that for the fifth Sunday after Epiphany, we ask Him "to keep His Church and household in His true religion;" and again, on the twenty-second Sunday after Trinity, we beg Him to keep His household, the Church, in continual godliness. The great Church catholic, then, is to be thought of, not only as God's kingdom, but as His family. It is under this latter aspect that I wish now to consider it.

A family is not "a fortuitous concourse of atoms." It consists of a number of members, either related by blood or united by a common purpose. Now the very idea of a member is that of a part of some organization differentiated or set apart for some office for which it is specially fitted by structure or position, or both. The very simplest living creature—the very germ cell from which the lowest seaweed is produced—has its parts so distinguished, and the higher we rise in the scale, the more striking are the differences. The family is an organism, and it follows that every member of the same has his own "vocation and ministry," which nobody can fulfill as well as himself. "The Lord has chosen him." (1 Chron. xxviii. 10.) He has appointed his place and set his task before him. Surely this is a great honor.

The great trouble is that the member thus appointed does not see his work, and he does not see it, for the most part, because he will not. Perhaps he thinks his appointed task too humble. He thinks it beneath his capacity. He is too often like a certain little girl, who was set by her mother to watch that the bread did not run over, but who thought it would be much finer to run the sewing machine. The result may easily be imagined. A woman who wished to undertake some Church work was invited to begin by taking a class from the infant room. She declined, saying that she would feel herself to be throwing away her time teaching such ignorant little ones. She was allowed to try a class of grown-up girls. She soon found out her mistake. She complained that the girls were always asking questions and making remarks, and at last she threw up the work in disgust, and there was the end of her aspirations after Church work. If she could only have had something congenial, she said, it would have been different.

Another church member was fired with enthusiasm on hearing an eloquent missionary sermon. She only wished that she could go out to Africa. That would, indeed, be worth while. But when it was suggested that she might give of an abundant wardrobe to help fill a missionary box, she rejected the idea with some tartness. She did not take so much pains with her things, to give them to a common negro preacher's wife !

There are several inconveniences resulting from this unwillingness or inability of the members of God's family to recognize and do their own work. One of them, and that not the least, is the loss to the member himself—a loss of opportunities of usefulness, and of growth in grace. The member which is never used in its appropriate office loses its vigor, and often becomes paralyzed beyond recovery. We have all heard of the East Indian devotees, who hold their hands above their heads till they grow into that position, and cannot be taken down ; and I have somewhere read of a nun who never used her hands, but kept them clasped in the attitude of prayer till the joints became useless. We think such conduct a horrible misuse of God's gifts, and rightly ; but we should do well to examine ourselves, lest we fall into the same error with respect to our spiritual faculties. But as a limb which has been partly paralyzed by misuse or disuse may often be restored by care and exercise, so no one need despair of regaining a good measure of usefulness, however faulty they may have been in the past.

Another trouble is that the uselessness of some members of the body throws additional work on the others. Everyone knows that when the skin refuses its office, the lungs and other bodily organs are overworked, and often become diseased in consequence. Think, for a moment, what would be the effect if the work of any ordinary parish were fairly divided among those who were able to do their share, though that share were ever so little. Suppose, for instance, that every woman who is able should lay by two cents a week for the women's auxiliary, and should devote one hour a week to working for it! Suppose that every man capable of teaching a class of boys should next Sunday offer to do so ! Suppose every church member who has not a valid excuse should be ready to undertake any piece of work pointed out by the rector ! A venerable saint of God once remarked that there were in almost every church two classes of willing members—a small class who were willing to do all the work, and a large class who were willing they should. How would the labors of the first class be lightened if the second class would awake to their duty!

Dear friends, let us examine ourselves whether we are doing our duty as members of the Church, which is the Lord's body. Let us see whether we have been shrinking or standing idly aside, and in the way of others, as idle folk almost always are. And if we find, after honest inquiry, that such has been the case, let us resolve that it shall be so no more. Let us ask forgiveness for all that is past, and with humility and docility strive hereafter, in the words of the catechism, "to do our duty in that state of life to which it shall please God to call us."

Neh. iv.   Rom. xii.

SIXTH WEDNESDAY IN LENT.

THE HOUSEHOLD OF GOD.—(*Continued.*)

ONE of the principal duties of the members of the household or family is loyalty—faithfulness to their head and to each other. The word covers a great deal. So far as our Great Head is concerned, it means obedience first of all—constant, unquestioning, cheerful obedience. That, and that alone, is the true test of our love ; as He Himself tells us : " He that hath my commandments and keepeth them, he it is that loveth Me." " He that loveth Me not, keepeth not my sayings." (S. John xiv. 21–24.) We are to obey, not when we feel like it, not when it is easy, not alone when we are in the society of fellow-disciples, but at all times, and in all places. Without such loyalty, no protestations of affection, no outbursts of enthusiasm, no efforts of church or missionary zeal, are of any value in the sight of our Master.

We are " to keep and *seek for* all the commandments of the Lord our God." (1 Chron.

xxviii. 8.) We are to study His written Word
diligently, and not only so, but we are to
watch carefully for indications of His will in
our every-day lives—for occasions of obedience and service.   There is not one of us but
can see, on looking back, a hundred occasions
of doing God service, which we have allowed
to pass unimproved simply from the want of
watchfulness.   The little events of our daily
lives are so many angel messengers bringing
words from our dear Head, but too often we
do not see their lovely faces, because we
never look at them till they have passed us
by.

The path of obedience is not always made
smooth and easy for us, any more than it
was for our Leader.   The gate is strait,
the path is narrow, the hills are high, the
waters deep. It was when the disciples were
crossing the lake in obedience to the Lord's
command that they met with the storm.   It
was when they were laboring in His cause
that they were to be scourged and stoned
and slandered by the very people they were
trying to benefit.   Our very carefulness and
zeal for Him may lead us into collision, yes,
even with our fellow-servants.   But what
then ?   The disciple is not above his Master,

nor the servant above his Lord. He has never promised us an easy journey. It is much that He has placed in our way many a living spring and many a flower and shady tree, and that He shows us, from time to time, from His Delectable Mountains, a view of that Celestial City which is to be our journey's end.

We are to be loyal not in deed only, but in word as well; and, strange as it may sound, I believe this latter kind of loyalty to be rather more rare than the former. There are many disciples who will obey the Master, often at a great sacrifice, who will never open their lips for Him. They will hear His name lightly spoken of, His claims derided or denied, and never open their mouths in His defense or to assert their own faith in Him. They will believe Him to be the only way of salvation, and yet never make one effort to bring to Him their servants, their work-peeple, even their own children. An officer who should behave in this way where the honor of his flag was concerned would have the straps torn from his shoulders. We need not sound a trumpet before us, nor make any parade of our own goodness; but we can, and we ought always, to own our allegiance

to Him, and to speak for Him. And to the
end that we may do this, we must take care
to walk so that our lives shall not contradict
our words, and that we may speak from our
own experience. "We have seen Him !" is
the argument which no infidel can answer.

Is. lviii.   S. John xiv.

SIXTH THURSDAY IN LENT.

THE HOUSEHOLD OF GOD.—Continued.

THE members of a family or household
owe a duty, not only to their head, but to
each other. They are bound in honor to
help one another when help is needed, to
sustain each other in trials, and to bear each
other's burdens; and the honor of one is the
honor of all, and the shame of one is the
shame of all.

So it is in the Church, which is the household of God. We are members of one body,
and so of each other. If one member suffers,
others suffer with it ; and not one can grow
in spiritual grace and strength without di-
rectly or indirectly benefiting others. If one
member is poor or afflicted in mind, body, or

estate, his fellows are bound to help him. If
he be assailed with slander or detraction,
the others are bound to defend him ; and so
on to the end of the chapter.

I suppose that no one—certainly no
church-member—will deny that these words
are true in theory; there are many, thank
God, to whom they are true in practice.
Would to God they were so to all! But,
alas! to how many are those with whom
they worship on Sunday, with whom they
kneel at the chancel rail even, of no more
real interest than the horses they pass in
the street. How many will sit next to a
person in church for years, and never ex-
change a greeting. How many actually
look down on their fellows who work for a
living, or who are not of their particular
set! A woman has been known to object
to the formation of a church guild because
" it would bring in everybody on an equal
footing. We would rather confine the thing
to our own set." It is to be hoped such ex-
treme instances are rare ; but that rector or
church worker is exceptionally happy who
has never found his efforts for the good of
the parish hampered by such feelings and
prejudices.

Again, a woman in poor or even moderate circumstances will not go to church herself, or send her children to Sunday-school, because she cannot dress herself or them as well as somebody with twice her means. She is always looking out for affronts, and resents every kindness and attention as an attempt at patronage.

Nor is this the worst. Members of the same church will not be content with neglect or mere passive envy. They will actually try to injure one another. It is a shame to have to say it, but it is true. A man or woman will kneel at the altar with another, and partake the emblems of their dying Saviour's love. They will do this, and then, before they are fairly out of sight of the church door, will repeat a scandalous story to that person's disadvantage—a story which they do not know to be true, and which there would be no use in telling if it were. Two communicants will quarrel, and keep up a grudge for years. I have known a person leave her parish church and go to another because, as she said, she could not go to the communion with such an one; as if the Lord's body were divided into parishes! So the Lord is shamed and wounded in the house of His friends, and the world says, ironically, "See how these Christians love one another!"

Oh, dear friends, fellow members of Christ, saved by the same infinite love and pity, washed in the same atoning blood, ought these things so to be? Are we not fasting for strife and debate when we pretend to keep Lent? Have we not all one Father? Has not God created us? "Why do we deal treacherously, every man against his brother?" (Mal. ii. 10.) Can the eye say to the hand, "I have no need of thee!" or, again, the head to the feet, "I have no need of you!" (1 Cor. xii. 21.) Can we wonder that the world does not care for the Church, while it sees the members of the church so indifferent, to say the least, to one another? Oh, let this holy season see every grudge renounced, every feeling of envy or pride put away, every quarrel made up! Let the blessed feast of Easter see us working and praying and loving as one in our risen Lord! So shall we be meet partakers of that Holy Table. So shall the power of the Church for good be increased a thousand-fold, and the Lord pour out a blessing till there shall be no room to receive it.

Mal. ii.   1 Cor. xii.

SIXTH FRIDAY IN LENT.

THE HOUSEHOLD OF GOD.—*Continued.*

WE must never forget that we are members of our Lord's great family, wherever we may be. The earthly family tie is not broken by absence, by distance, or even by death. The brother in California, the father on the distant frontier, are the brother and father still, followed by faithful prayers, by fond wishes, and remembered with tender tears at every family anniversary. Even though the wanderer be a prodigal as well, though it come to this, that his name is never heard, yet he is not forgotten. His place is empty, and must remain so, because it can be filled by none but himself. He may have forgotten his duty and renounced his family name, but the tie of blood is still there, and he cannot break it if he would.

It is so in the Household of God. Once a member, always a member. We may wander away, we may ignore our duties and forget our birthright ; like the prodigal, we may journey into a far country and waste our substance—which is not ours, but our Father's—with riotous living ; but though rebellious, we are His children still. But not to speak of that case at present, let us look a little at one or two others. You, my friend, have not been to church in months, perhaps years. You are shut up by illness or infirmity, and cannot go into the house of the Lord. It is a great misfortune, no doubt ; and yet it is not as bad as it might be. You are not cut off from the Lord's family, nor even from the services of the sanctuary. With your Bible and prayer-book you can follow the Church services throughout the Christian year. Some kind friend will keep you informed of the work that is going on in the parish, and you may perhaps be able now and then to give it a little help. Your church paper or missionary magazine will tell you the news of the Church at large, and you can at least follow with your prayers the good enterprises of which the time is so full. And if you cannot go to the Holy Communion, your pastor will gladly bring it to you. It is a wonder to me that invalids do not oftener avail themselves of this great privilege. Many persons seem to think it a service reserved for dying hours. " Has your sister had the Holy Communion since she was sick ? " was the question asked of an intelligent English woman. "Oh, no !" was the answer, in a tone of surprise, " we do not think her in any danger." It is to be feared that too many look on this ordinance as a kind of magic rite, by which they are somehow to be bewitched into Heaven at last, however they may have neglected it in their lifetime.

To those who are by absence deprived of the services of our Church I would say the same. Never allow yourself to forget your church ties, any more than you would forget your family relations on account of absence, but cherish them all the more. I would not have you stay away from the public worship of your fellow Christians, or refuse to help them in their good works. On the contrary, I would have you assist them in every possible way, and maintain the most friendly relations with them. But never, *never* forget your own household of faith. If possible let no Sunday or holy-day pass without joining in her worship. Work for her, pray for her, speak for her, at all proper times. How often has it happened that one such faithful member has been the seed from which has grown a vine bearing fruit unto eternal life ! You cannot be deprived of all church privileges so long as you have your prayer-book, and if you use faithfully what you have, the Lord will send you others. Above all things, never allow yourself to forget that you are a member of the Lord's body.

It is possible that this book may fall into the hands of some one who has forgotten his birthright, who, like the Scripture prodigal, has gone into a far country, and is trying to satisfy the hunger of his soul with the husks of this world—with money or land, or low, vile pleasures fit only for swine. To such an one let me say, your place in your Father's house and heart and table is still open to you. No one has taken it. No one ever will take it. It stands waiting for you, and unless you come home to occupy it, it must stand forever empty. Oh, my brother, my sister, remember that you are still God's child ! You must be so, you cannot help yourself. Rebellious you may be, disobedient, ungrateful, lost to love, even to shame; you are still the child of God. Even though you have never been baptized in His name. He created you, and He has cared for you all these years. Return, then, to His House and His love while there is yet time, lest at last the door should be shut, and you be left to yourself, an orphan in the universe.

Dan. iv.   St. Luke xv.

SATURDAY BEFORE PALM SUNDAY.

THE ALABASTER BOX.

THE selections of Holy Scripture set forth for the days of Holy Week are so abundant and so important that any one who studies them as they deserve will have little time for any other reading.* I propose, therefore, merely to glance at some one event of each particular day, following the chronology adopted by Dean Farrar.

After the excitement which followed the raising of Lazarus, our Lord withdrew from Jerusalem to a little city called Ephraim, on the edge of the desert, where He seems to have spent some weeks in quiet and restful retirement with His disciples. Six days be-

* For the same reason I have named no selections from the Bible.

fore the Passover He returned to the neighborhood of Jerusalem. He did not, however, enter the city immediately, but betook Himself to the little village of Bethany, the home of His chosen friends Mary and Martha, and their brother Lazarus. It was at a supper made for their honored guest that Mary's full heart overflowed in that offering which has made her name sweet through all the ages, and on which her Lord bestowed the emphatic commendation, "She hath done what she could."

She hath done what she could! She gave her Lord the very best of all that she possessed—the alabaster vase of precious perfume, costly as gold; an article of luxury, even with the rich. Are we doing the same? Do we give Him the best of our time, our means, our labors? Or do we, like the covetous Jews rebuked by the prophet, offer Him only that which no one else will thank us for? "Cursed be the deceiver who hath in his flock a male, and voweth and sacrificeth unto the Lord a corrupt thing." (Mal. i. xiii.)

She hath done what she could! If she had been able to offer no more than a bunch of sweet herbs gathered in the fields, we cannot doubt that the offering would have been as acceptable to the Lord of earth and sky as the costly ointment. He to whom belong the cattle upon a thousand hills was as well pleased with the turtle doves—the sacrifice of the very poorest—as with the oxen and sheep of the prince in Israel. Let us never hesitate to give what we can because the gift is small.

She hath done what she could! It was her love which made the offering acceptable. She first gave herself (2 Cor. viii. 5), and the rest followed, as a matter of course. Let us honestly offer and present to the Lord ourselves, our souls and bodies, our powers, our very weakness and hindrances, and having done so, let us, as some old divine says, " keep ourselves on the altar," taking back nothing of all that we have given. The altar shall sanctify the gift, and make it as worthy of our Lord's accceptance as was Mary's box of precious perfume.

PALM SUNDAY.

CHILDREN IN THE TEMPLE.

THE great event of the day was over. The Lord had come to Jerusalem, fulfilling the words of the prophet. His had been a triumphal entry, and for a little time it seemed, indeed, as if the world had gone after Him. Only He Himself knew how evanescent would be the feeling in his favor. Only He knew that some of the very tongues which had cried "Hosanna!" would in no long time be as ready to cry, "Crucify Him!"

But there were other voices—innocent voices—to which the Lord could listen with delight. The little children in the temple, who had followed Him thither with their parents—possibly also those employed in the musical service—continued to repeat the shouts of the multitudes on the Mount of Olives, and the spacious courts resounded with their shrill hosannas. His enemies were all the more enraged, and would have silenced them, but the Lord refused, and justified their action. "Yea, have ye never

12

heard, Out of the mouth of babes and suck-
lings Thou hast perfected praise " ?

Nowadays the children's place in the temple is too often vacant. One sees but seldom
what was once the most common of Sunday
sights—the long, orderly rows of children,
big and little, filling the pews on Sunday. I
cannot recollect when I first went to church,
but I well remember what a deprivation it
was to be kept at home.   If the morning
service was thought too long for the very
little ones, they were taken in the afternoon.
But the afternoon service has been turned
into the evening, when the children cannot
come out (it being considered by careful
mothers much more dangerous to take them
to church than to dancing-school); and at
the morning service the clergyman may look
over twenty pews and not see half a dozen
children.

Surely this is not right. Surely the praises
of the little ones are as acceptable now as
they were on the first Palm Sunday. Children soon learn to understand and join in
the service. I shall never forget being, many
years ago, in a church where the responses
were made so faintly that one might think
the worshippers were afraid some one would

hear them. All at once, in the midst of that cold, dying murmur, arose distinct and clear the voice of a little child saying in devoutest accents, " Good Lord, deliver us." All through the Litany the sweet little tones were heard, and it was curious to hear how others near him found courage to open their mouths.

Dear friends, let us take the children to church. Let us not deprive them of their birthright. Their place is in the Sanctuary as well as ours, and they will soon learn to consider worship a privilege. They will learn to love God's house when they are young, and when they are old they will not depart from it.

MONDAY BEFORE EASTER.

THE FIG-TREE HAVING LEAVES.

THE Lord had, as usual, gone out of the city to spend the night. He seems to have had no love for cities in general. He had spent the dark hours either at Bethany, or, as is very probable, He had slept with His disciples in the open air, under the trees of the

Mount of Olives. All Orientals are rather fond of sleeping out of doors, and a night on the grass, wrapped in their big mantles, is, to them, no hardship at all. But returning to Jerusalem early in the morning, He was an-hungered; and seeing a fig-tree having leaves, He came to it, if possibly He might find fruit thereon.

The time of figs—the general harvest—had not yet come. But this particular tree had put on its summer dress of leaves ; and therefore it was reasonable to expect that it should also bear fruit, since the fruit of the fig-tree always precedes the leaf. Our Lord might have expected to find some of the small green figs which there often come to perfection in April or May.* But the tree was barren. It had not even remaining any of the large purple fruit which hangs on till the next season. It was barren now ; it had been barren the year before. And so the Lord pronounced its condemnation. " Let no fruit grow on thee henceforth forever."

Is there a possibility that one of us who

---

*NOTE.—Thomson, author of " The Land and the Book" (which ought to be in every Sunday-school library as a book of reference), speaks of eating the little sweet green figs as early as April.

have followed the Church services all through this holy season may be, after all, like this fig-tree? It is possible that we may be like the empty vine described by the prophet— empty because it brought forth fruit only to itself? (Hos. x. 1.) Oh, let us look to it, lest our Lord, seeking for fruit and finding none, may pronounce against us also the awful sentence, "No fruit grow on thee henceforth forever."

TUESDAY BEFORE EASTER.

THE HOUSE LEFT DESOLATE.

OUR Lord had visited the temple for the last time. He had silenced all his enemies; He had frustrated all their deep-laid plans to entangle Him in His own words. He had poured out on the Scribes and Pharisees those terrible denunciations which filled up the cup of their spite and fury to overflowing. Then looking about Him, doubtless, at the magnificent building, and the still great and prosperous city with its crowded inhabitants, His heart of love and pity overflowed once more, as it had done at the time of His triumphal entry. "O Jerusalem, Jerusalem, thou that killest the prophets and stonest them that are sent unto thee, how often would I have gathered thy children together, as a hen gathereth her chickens under her wings, and ye would not." And then came the saddest words of all. "Behold, your house is left unto you, desolate."

Our Lord never entered the temple again. It stood in its majesty for many a year, untouched by any outward enemy, throwing back the sunbeams, a "pile of gold and snow." Yet was it as surely a ruin as when the fire that devoured it was quenched in the blood of priests and worshippers. For the Lord had departed and all the splendor was but an empty show. The house was left, but it was desolate.

Probably none of those who crowded to hear the Lord's last words, realized that they were the last. He had been going in and out among them for three years. They had become, as it were, used to seeing His miracles and hearing His teachings, and there seemed no special reason why these miracles and teachings should not go on indefinitely. Probably very few, except His bitterest enemies, had made up their minds absolutely to reject Him. There was time enough, they thought.

But they were awfully mistaken. There was no more time. The clock had struck, though they had not heard it. The Lord, whom they had pretended to seek, had come to His temple, but the rulers there would have none of Him. And so they were left to themselves, to fill up the measure of their iniquities, and to be filled in turn with their own devices in a manner more awful than the world has ever seen.

To every man and woman on earth there is coming a last time—a last Lent, a last Easter, a last Sunday, a last chance. " God had appointed a day." We know not what day, nor when it is to come, but being appointed, it is constantly drawing nearer and nearer. And when once the Master of the house has risen, and has shut to the door, it will not be opened again. God grant that at that awful time, none of us who have walked on together through this holy season, may be left outside that door to knock in vain!

WEDNESDAY BEFORE EASTER.

THE LOST OPPORTUNITIES.

WE may think of this day with tender interest as our Lord's last quiet day upon
earth.   He seems to have spent it in retirement with His disciples, probably among
the groves of that Mount which He loved so
well ; not yet invaded by the foot of treach-
ery and violence, but lying sweet and calm
and beautiful with the tender tints of spring.
Here He told His friends of the terrible fate
which was even then threatening that temple, to whose beauty and strength they had
so lately directed His attention, and of that
still more awful event, also inevitable, but
the date whereof was still hidden in the
councils of God. At this time, too, He spoke
the parables of the wise and foolish virgins,
and of the talents, and gave the description
of the last Judgment contained in the same
chapter.

It is on one feature of the narration in
this chapter that I would dwell for a few

minutes. The most startling and significant thing about them all has always seemed to me this : that in every case the persons condemned were so condemned not for what they did, but for what they did not do. The foolish virgins made no bad use of their lamps. They did not willfully waste their oil for their own pleasure. They simply neglected to provide it when they might have done so. When the time came that the lamps were needed they hastened to supply the deficiency, but it was then too late. They that were ready had gone in to the marriage, and the door was shut.

So it was with the slothful servant with his one talent. He made no ill use of it. We do not hear that he drank or gambled. He was slothful—perhaps cowardly as well. So he hid his Lord's money, and was judged accordingly. The man with one talent is perhaps specially exposed to this temptation. He can do but little in comparison to others, and so he will do nothing. But if his sentence was so severe, what shall be that of him who, having ten talents given him to serve his master withal, lets them lie unimproved, or uses them for his own and others' destruction.

Again, in the story of judgment, with which the chapter concludes, those who were sent away to the place prepared, not for them, but for the devil and his angels, were condemned, not because they had ill-treated or robbed any one, but because having the opportunity to succor the Lord in the persons of His poor, they had not done so.

Do not these stories contain an awful warning ? How many say, if not openly, yet to themselves, "At least, if I do no good, I do no great harm." But let us not be deceived. The not doing good is of itself a sin, and as a sin it will surely be visited.

THURSDAY BEFORE EASTER.

THE TRAITOR.

" WHEN evening was come, He sat down with the twelve" to the meal already prepared by the two disciples whom He had sent in the morning for that purpose. We cannot tell what were the thoughts that then occupied His mind, any further than the Holy Spirit had revealed them to us, but, so far, we may without presumption humbly try to enter into them. He knew, though His disciples did not, that his enemies were awake, and already planning His destruction, and that one of His chosen companions, who was breaking bread with Him, would betray Him into their hands. He saw all the weakness and folly of those companions, even then disputing who should be greatest; He foresaw their cowardly desertion and flight. His soul was sorrowful, even unto death; yet we hear no words of impatience; only solemn warnings and tender counsels.

There was one of the number to whom every look should have been a reproach, every word a sting. He had sold his Lord already, and was only biding his time to consummate the bargain; yet he could sit there at the board, could take the bread from that Master's own hand, could even ask with the others, "Is it I?"

Did his conscience even then torment him? Probably not. He had hardened it too long. Says a well-known writer: "Remorse may disturb the slumber of a man who is dabbling with his first experiences of wrong; and when the pleasure has been tasted and is gone, and nothing is left of the crime but the ruin it has wrought, then, too, the furies take their seats upon the midnight pillow. But the meridian of evil is for the most part left unvexed, and when a man has chosen his road he is left alone to follow it to the end." Judas had chosen his road. He had sold his Master for a paltry sum of money, and probably pleased himself with the thoughts of farther advantages which would be certain to follow such a service to the rulers. The world had hidden all else from his eyes, and if he now and then had a misgiving, he doubtless stifled it with the thought that the Master who had so often escaped the hands of his enemies would easily do so again. He would have the money and the credit, and there would be no great harm done after all.

Is there any danger now, that Judas may be found at the Lord's table? Is there any danger that we may betray our Master for gold, for fashion, or for worldly advantage? Do we ever, for the sake of being thought liberal or intellectual, side with His open or covert enemies?

Let us beware! It was an awful distinction which our merciful and compassionate Lord gave to Judas. There was pardon for those who forsook Him for fear, for Peter who denied, for Paul who persecuted. It was only Judas who sold Him, of whom it was said, " It were better for that man that he had never been born ! "

GOOD FRIDAY.

THE CROSS.

THERE seems to be no room on this day for human words. What we have to do is to follow our suffering Lord step by step through the events of the day ; to see Him led from the high priest to Pilate, from Pilate to Herod, and back to Pilate again ; to see the cowardly Roman governor, acting against his own sense of law and justice for fear of the mob, seeking to save the innocent by a compromise, which failed, as such compromises always do, and at last giving way and delivering the victim into the hands of his enemies, to find, after all, that he had gained nothing but infamy by the surrender of honor and conscience. Let us, with the daughters of Jerusalem, follow the sad procession to Calvary. Let us see the Saviour of the world fainting under His burden, yet forgetting His own pain to address to the wailing women a word of recognition and warning. Let us see Him refusing the narcotic provided by merciful hands to deaden the agonies of the sufferers. Let us, with His mother and the other faithful women, watch by His cross to the end. Surely we can do this for Him who has done so much for us. And as we keep our sorrowful yet joyful watch, let us always remember that *we* have our part in that awful sacrifice ; that *our* sins made a part of that crushing burden ; that our sins sharpened the nails and embittered the cup. Let us say again and again, as we watch the shadow darkening on the Saviour's brow, that shadow which never anywhere falls but once, " He died for me! "

He died for you, oh timid, doubting, desponding soul. How, then, can you distrust your Father's love, who suffered His well-beloved Son to bear all this for your sake ? He died for you, oh weak and weary sufferer, and He who so bore His own cross will help you to bear yours. Oh, thoughtless or careless sinner, or hardened man of the world; oh, blasphemer or denier! He died for you that you might live for Him. Let it not be in vain that He has so died !

EASTER EVEN.

THE LAST SABBATH.

THE agony was over at last. Joseph and Nicodemus, openly taking sides with the disciples of Jesus in this their darkest hour, had begged the Lord's body, and with all the tenderness and reverence which the time admitted, had laid it safely away in the garden tomb. The faithful women who had watched by the cross saw where the body of their Lord was laid, and sadly returned home. There was no more that they could do. Yes, one thing more. They prepared spices and ointments, and then, anxious as they were to complete the last service they could show, they rested the Sabbath day according to the commandment. If they could do no more, they could obey that law which He Himself had said should not pass away till all was fulfilled.

They rested the Sabbath day. A sorrowful day, no doubt, yet not perhaps without its gleams of comfort. He whom they trusted was to redeem Israel was gone, dead by a shameful and cruel death. After all His faithful teaching for three years among them, after all His miracles, after that triumphal entry of only a week before, He was dead. And yet, as they who had followed Him so faithfully talked over the events of their Lord's life, and recalled His words, it seems as if they must have remembered those mysterious words of His about rising again. How many had He not recalled from death ? Had He not brought Lazarus back after he had been dead four days ? At all events, He was now out of reach of His enemies. Their malice could not harm Him now, and they should see Him again at that resurrection of the just which He had taught them to expect.

They rested the Sabbath day according to the commandment. It was, though they did not know it then, the last Sabbath under the old law. Henceforth, as long as the world stood, the first instead of the last day of the week was to be the " day of rest and gladness " to all Christian hearts and homes. It was to be pre-eminently the Lord's day— Sunday, we may well call it, since on that day the Sun of Righteousness rose on His

Church to set no more. The disciples and the women did not know that it was the last, but they kept it in obedience. That at least was in their power.

It may be that some one who reads these pages is bowed down with trouble from within or without ; perplexed with doubt, burdened with a sense of unworthiness, and hesitating whether or not to go to the Easter feast. To such an one let me say, dear friend, you can always obey. The King Himself invites you to the feast; and a royal invitation is a command. Draw near with faith, and take what your King offers you out of loyalty to His will. Believe me, He will himself give you the wedding garment which shall render you fit for His presence. And as for your burden, lay it at His feet and leave it there. Only obey, and the blessing will as surely follow as light follows the sun.

EASTER.

THE DAY OF THE LORD.

THIS is the day of the Lord ; we will rejoice and be glad in it. It is the great day of the Church, the crowning feast of the year. Even the world rejoices on Christmas Day, though it scarcely knows why; but this is the Christian's day. To him who does not believe, it means nothing ; to us, it means everything.

Our Lord has risen from the dead. Henceforth the grave has for us no terror. Our Lord has opened its fast-barred gates and let in the sunshine to every corner ; and as we look into it, we see nothing to affright us. He has made it a safe resting-place; and we may commit to it the bodies of our dear ones, with the tears that love demands indeed, but in hope, because as our Lord rose they too shall rise to die no more.

Our Lord is risen from the dead; and from henceforth the hope of a future life is no more a dream, a theory, a fond hope. To us who believe, it is a certainty beyond all doubt. Because He lives, we shall live also.

When the women and the other disciples had become assured that their Lord had really risen; when He had spoken and eaten with them, and their hands had touched and handled Him, the distress and grief of the last few days must have seemed to them like a bad dream. So will the longest, weariest life seem to the disciple who looks at it from the rest of Paradise. It was long, but the end came at last. It was hard to bear, but it is all over now. The poor, weak soul trembled at the passage, but it was safely made, and the Home is gained, from which there is no going out forevermore. It was a dark, restless night perhaps, full of sad dreams and fears, but it is past and gone now. The sun has risen, and it will never set.

Our Lord is risen from the dead! He calls us, as He did His disciples, to eat and drink with Him. Let us hasten to obey. And if we are so shut in that we cannot go with the multitude to His holy table, let us prepare Him a place in our hearts, and rest assured that He will come and sup with us and we with Him.

CONCLUSION.

LOOKING BACK.

EVERY wise merchant, at the close of a busy season, looks back over his business, and reckons up his profits and losses. We, dear friends, have been passing through a season of more than usual occupation and privilege. Lent is now at an end. Let us look back and see if we have gained or lost ground in our spiritual progress during the last busy days.

We have surely gained, if we have used them as we ought. If we have laid out a plan of work or study or self-denial, and ad-hered to it as far as possible, our wills have been strengthened by the process. If we have taken unavoidable interruptions pleas-antly, if we have borne with criticism, kind or unkind, good-naturedly, if we have been un-ostentatious in our devotions, while yielding not a jot of what we believe to be right, we have surely grown in grace. If we have laid aside light and amusing books, that we might have more time for religious reading and for Bible study, we have increased in knowledge. In short, if we have used the time as we ought, we have laid up strength and formed good habits which will help us through the entire year.

But if, through idleness or self-indulgence, we have allowed the precious hours and days to pass empty away ; if our Bibles have been neglected, and our time frittered away on trifles; if we have done and given nothing for the spread of the Gospel, the advancement of the Lord's cause—then has the Lenten season been lost. If we have formed no good habits to carry us through the rest of the year, if we are ready to plunge into new frivolities, or to take up the old ones with a new zest after a few weeks of abstinence, then it is worse than lost. We might better not have had it. For every privilege misused, every means of grace unimproved, does but harden the heart and blunt the conscience.

Without wishing to be censorious, it does seem to me that a good many Christians do up their religion in Lent, so as to have little left for the rest of the year. For six weeks they are to be seen in the Sunday-school, at the missionary meeting, at the week-day service; but look for them after Easter, and you will find their places vacant. "Yes, I went to the meetings in Lent," said one ; " but now that the world is going on again, there are so many claims on my time !" One could not help wondering a little what claims the world had on the time of a Christian after Easter any more than before.

But let us beware of judging our neighbors; we shall have quite enough to do in examining our own consciences and bewailing our own sinfulness, that we may come well prepared to the blessed feast of Easter. We shall all see plenty to regret in the weeks that are past. Let us see to it that the coming days—the days of our Lord's humiliation and death—are so employed as that the feast of His joyful and glorious resurrection may find us ready, in the marriage garment prescribed by Holy Scripture, to be meet partakers of that Holy Table.

Isa. liii. 1 Cor. xi. 17.

THE END.